Little Jewel

English translations of works by Patrick Modiano

From Yale University Press

After the Circus

Little Jewel

Paris Nocturne

Pedigree

Suspended Sentences

Also available or forthcoming

The Black Notebook

Catherine Certitude

Dora Bruder

Honeymoon

In the Café of Lost Youth

Lacombe Lucien

Missing Person

Out of the Dark

So You Don't Get Lost in the Neighborhood

The Occupation Trilogy (The Night Watch, Ring Roads, and La Place de l'Etoile)

Villa Triste

Young Once

Little Jewel

Patrick Modiano

Translated from the French
by Penny Hueston

Yale UNIVERSITY PRESS • NEW HAVEN AND LONDON

A MARGELLOS
WORLD REPUBLIC OF LETTERS BOOK

The Margellos World Republic of Letters is dedicated to making literary works from around the globe available in English through translation. It brings to the English-speaking world the work of leading poets, novelists, essayists, philosophers, and playwrights from Europe, Latin America, Africa, Asia, and the Middle East to stimulate international discourse and creative exchange.

Yale University Press books may be purchased in quantity for educational, business, or promotional use. For information, please e-mail sales.press@yale.edu (U.S. office) or sales@yaleup.co.uk (U.K. office).

Page design by W. H. Chong.
Typeset by J & M Typesetting.
Cover design by James J. Johnson.
Printed in the United States of America.

Library of Congress Control Number: 2016933155
ISBN 978-0-300-22182-4 (hardcover: alk. paper)

A catalogue record for this book is available from the British Library.

This paper meets the requirements of ANSI/NISO Z39.48-1992 (Permanence of Paper).

10 9 8 7 6 5 4 3 2 1

For Zina *For Marie*

IT MUST HAVE been about twelve years since anyone had called me Little Jewel. I found myself at Châtelet metro station at peak hour. I was in the crowd heading along the endless corridor on the moving walkway. There was a woman wearing a yellow coat. The colour of the coat caught my eye and I observed her from the back on the walkway. Then she headed down the corridor marked DIRECTION CHÂTEAU DE VINCENNES. Now we were all squashed against each other in the middle of the staircase, waiting for the barrier to open. She was standing next to me. I saw her face. She was so like my mother that I thought it must be her.

I remembered one of the few photos I have kept of my mother. It's as if a searchlight trained on her face had made it loom out of the darkness. I've always felt uneasy looking at this photo. Every time it appeared in my dreams, it was like an identikit photo that someone was showing me—a police superintendent, an employee at the morgue—so that I could identify this person.

I did not say a word. I knew nothing about the woman. She sat down on one of the benches in the station, away from the people jostling on the edge of the platform while they waited for the train. There was no room on the bench next to her; I stood to the side, leaning against a vending machine. Her coat had no doubt been fashionable at one time and its colour gave it a touch of flair. But the yellow had faded almost to grey. She seemed oblivious to everything around her and I wondered if she would stay there all evening, on the bench, until the last metro. She had the same profile as my mother, that distinctive nose, slightly upturned. The same bright eyes. The same high forehead. Her hair was shorter. She hadn't changed much. Her hair was not as blonde anymore, but, after all, I had no idea if my mother had been a true blonde. Her mouth was set in a bitter grimace. I was certain it was her.

She let a train go past. The platform was empty for a few minutes. I sat down on the bench next to her. Then another dense crowd swarmed onto the platform. I could have struck up a conversation with her. I couldn't find the words and there were too many people around us.

She was about to fall asleep on the bench but, when the noise of the next train was still only a distant rumbling, she got to her feet. I stepped into the carriage, just behind her. We were separated by a group of men who were speaking loudly to each other. The doors shut and that's when I realised I should have taken the train going in the other direction, as I normally did. At the next station, I was pushed onto the platform by the tide of people alighting, then I stepped back into the carriage and moved over to stand next to her.

In the stark light, she looked older than she had on the platform. Her left temple and part of her cheek were scarred. How old was she? Fifty or so? And how old was she in the photos? Twenty-five? Her expression was the same as when she was twenty-five, clear, revealing astonishment or an intimation of fear, and abruptly hardening. Her gaze happened to land on me, but she didn't see me. She took a powder compact out of her coat pocket and opened it. She brought the mirror up to her face and ran the little finger of her left hand over the corner of her eyelid, as if she were wiping away a speck of dust. The train was speeding up, there was a jolt, I grabbed the metal railing, but she didn't lose her balance. She remained impassive, staring at herself in the mirror. At Bastille, everyone somehow managed to get in, and the doors had trouble shutting. She had time to put away her compact before the new passengers poured into the carriage.

What station was she going to get off at? Would I follow her all the way? Was it really necessary? I had to get used to the idea that she lived in the same city as I did. I'd been told that she had died, a long time ago, in Morocco, and I'd never tried to find out anything more. 'She died in Morocco': one of those set phrases from childhood. I never really knew what it meant. A set phrase that echoes in the memory, like certain words from songs that used to frighten me. 'There was once a little boat…' 'She died in Morocco.' Her date of birth was entered on my birth certificate—1917—and, at the time the photos were taken, she claimed to be twenty-five. But she must have already been lying about her age and falsifying her papers in order to appear younger.

She turned up the collar of her coat as if she were feeling cold in the carriage, and yet we were all jammed in next to one another. I could see that the edge of her collar was frayed. How long had she been wearing that coat? Ever since the photos were taken? That's why the yellow had faded. We were arriving at the end of the line and, from there, a bus would take us to a distant suburb. I'd approach her then. After Gare de Lyon, the carriage was less crowded. Once again, her gaze landed on me, but it was that look which passengers exchange unthinkingly. *Do you remember they used to call me Little Jewel? You, too, went by another name back then. And even your first name, Sonia, was made up.*

Now we were sitting opposite each other on the banquettes closest to the doors. *I tried to find you in the phone book and I even telephoned four or five people with the same surname, but they had never heard of you. I told myself that one day I would go to Morocco. It was the only way to verify whether you were in fact dead.*

After Nation the carriage was empty, but she was still there, sitting opposite me, her hands clasped and the sleeves of the discoloured coat revealing her wrists. Bare, chapped hands, without rings or bracelets. In the photos, she was wearing bracelets and rings—clunky jewellery popular at the time. But these days, nothing. She had shut her eyes. Three more stops and it would be the end of the line. The train would terminate at Château de Vincennes, and I would stand up as gently as possible, and get out of the carriage, leaving her asleep on the seat. I would take the other train, in the direction of Pont de Neuilly, as I would have done had I not noticed that yellow coat in the corridor.

The train pulled into Bérault station. She opened her eyes, which had taken on that hard glare again. She glanced at the platform, and stood up. Once again, I followed her along the corridor, but now we were alone. Then I noticed she was wearing those knitted slipper socks called *panchos*, which accentuated her dancer's gait.

A wide avenue, lined with apartment buildings, on the border between Vincennes and Saint-Mandé. Night was falling. She crossed the avenue and went into a phone box. I waited for the lights to change a few times, and then I crossed, too. In the phone box, she took a while to find change or a token. I feigned interest in the window of the nearest shop, a chemist displaying the poster that terrified me in my childhood: the devil blowing fire out of his mouth. I turned away. She dialled a number slowly, as if for the first time, and then held the receiver against her ear with both hands. But there was no answer. She hung up. She took a bit of paper out of one of her coat pockets and stared at it while her finger dialled. That's when

I wondered whether she had a home somewhere.

This time, someone replied. Behind the pane of glass, her lips were moving. She was again holding the receiver with both hands and, from time to time, she shook her head, as if to focus her attention. From the movement of her lips, she was speaking louder and louder, more vehemently, but eventually she calmed down. Who could she possibly be calling? Among the few remaining things of hers in my possession, inside a metal biscuit tin, were a diary and an address book from the period of the photos, back when I was called Little Jewel. When I was younger, I had no interest in looking at the diary or the address book, but for some time now, in the evenings, I would turn the pages. Names. Telephone numbers. I knew there was no point in dialling the numbers. What's more, I had no desire to.

In the phone box, she kept talking. She seemed so engrossed by the conversation that I drew nearer without her noticing me. I even pretended to be waiting for my turn to use the telephone. I thought I might catch a few words that would help me to understand better what this woman in the yellow coat and slipper socks had become. But I couldn't hear a thing through the glass. Perhaps she was calling one of the people in the address book, the only one she hadn't lost contact with, or who hadn't died. Often, there's someone who remains a constant presence in your life, someone you can't ever shake off, someone who got to know you in the good times but is still there beside you when you're down and out, still supportive, the last true believer, with the blind faith of a simpleton. A no-hoper like you. A devoted friend. Forever the punching bag. I tried to imagine what this man, or woman, at the other end of the line might look like.

She came out of the phone box. She looked at me idly, the same look she'd given me in the metro. I opened the glass door. Without dropping a token in the slot, I dialled a number at random, for no reason, waiting for her to move away. I kept the receiver against my ear, even though there wasn't a dial tone. Silence. I couldn't find the resolve to hang up.

She went into the café next to the chemist. I hesitated before following her, but decided that she wouldn't notice me. Who were we, the two of us? A woman of indeterminate age and a young woman, both lost in the crowd in the metro. No one would have been able to single us out. And, when we surfaced outside, we were just like the thousands and thousands of people who return to their neighbourhoods every evening.

She was sitting at a table at the back. The chubby blond barman had brought her a kir. I would have to check whether she came here every evening, at the same time. I was determined to remember the name of the café. Le Calciat, 96 Avenue de Paris. The name was written in white letters in a semicircle on the glass door. In the metro, on the way back, I repeated the name and address to myself, over and over, so I could write it down as soon as possible. There was no death in Morocco. The secret life continued. A kir every evening at Le Calciat and the other patrons got used to seeing the woman in the yellow coat. No one thought twice about her.

I sat down at a table not far from hers. I ordered a kir, too, raising my voice so she might hear, hoping she would take it as a sign of complicity. But she remained impassive. Her head was slightly tilted, her expression at once severe and wistful, her arms folded, leaning on the table, the same pose as in the painting. Whatever happened to that painting? It followed me around during my childhood. It was hanging in my bedroom in Fossombronne-la-Forêt. 'That's the portrait of your mother,' I was told. A fellow called Tola Soungouroff had painted it in Paris. The name and the city were written in the bottom left-hand corner. Her arms were folded, like they were now, though she was wearing a heavy chain-link bracelet around one wrist. That was my pretext for starting a conversation. *You look just like a woman whose portrait I saw last week at the flea market in Porte de Clignancourt. The painter's name was Tola Soungouroff.* But I couldn't find the wherewithal to get up and go over to her, even assuming I were able to get the words out without making a mistake: *The painter's name was Tola Soungouroff, and your first name, Sonia, was made up; the real one, as it appears on my birth certificate, was Suzanne.* But, once I'd raced through that sentence, how would it make anything clearer for me? She would pretend not to understand, or else she'd stumble over her words, and they'd come out all jumbled, because she hadn't talked to anyone for so long. Or she would lie, she would cover her tracks, like she did at the time of the portrait and the photos, by lying about her age and by giving a false first name. And surname. And even a false title of nobility. She used to let people believe that she had been born into a family from the Irish aristocracy. She must have had dealings with an Irishman, otherwise she would never have come up with that idea. An Irishman. My father, perhaps—who would be difficult to track down, and whom she must have forgotten. She had probably forgotten everything else, and would be surprised that I had raised it with her. That person was someone else, not her. The lies had dissolved over time. But I was sure that, back then, she believed every last one of them.

The chubby blond barman brought her another kir. Now there were a lot of people standing at the bar. And all the tables were full. We would not have been able to hear each other in the hubbub. I had the feeling that I was still on the metro. Or, rather, in the waiting room of a station, without knowing exactly which train to catch. She was putting off going home. It probably wasn't far away. I was genuinely curious to know where she lived. I had no desire at all to speak to her; I felt nothing in particular towards her. Circumstances had prevented us from sharing what people call the milk of human kindness. The only thing I wanted to know was where she had washed up, twelve years after her death in Morocco.

IT WAS A little street near the Château de Vincennes or its fort. I'm not exactly sure what the difference is between the two. The street was lined with single-storey houses, garages and even stables. Indeed, it was called Rue du Quartier-de-Cavalerie. In the middle, on the right-hand side, a large dark-brick apartment block stood out. Night had fallen by the time we stepped onto the street. I was still walking a few steps behind her, but little by little I reduced the distance between us. I was certain that, even if I walked level with her, she wouldn't notice me.

I revisited this street later, during the day. You headed past the brick apartment block, and were going to end up in a wasteland. There was not a cloud in the sky. When you got to the end of the street, it opened onto a sort of vacant lot, which bordered a much larger area. There was a sign: ARMY OPERATIONS. Beyond that was the Bois de Vincennes park.

But, at night, this street looked like any other suburban street: Asnières, Issy-les-Moulineaux, Levallois...She was moving slowly, with her dancer's walk. It mustn't have been easy in slipper socks.

The dark mass of the apartment block dominated all the other buildings. Why was it here, in this street? On the ground floor there was a grocery store about to close for the night. The fluorescent lighting had been turned off and the only light was at the cash register. Through the glass I could see her taking food off the back shelves, one can, then another. And a black packet. Coffee? Chicory? She clutched the cans and the packet against her coat but, once she got to the register, she fumbled. The cans and the packet tumbled to the ground. The fellow at the register picked them up. He smiled at her. Their lips were moving, and I would have liked to know what name he called her. Her true, unmarried name? She left, cradling the cans and the packet against her coat with both hands, as if she were carrying a newborn baby. I almost offered to help, but Rue du Quartier-de-Cavalerie suddenly seemed like a backwater, a long way from Paris, in a garrison town. Soon everything would be shut, the town would be deserted, and I would miss the last train.

She went through the metal gate. The minute I saw this dark-brick building, I had an intuition that she lived there. She crossed the courtyard, at the end of which were several identical apartment blocks. She was walking more and more slowly, perhaps frightened that she would drop her shopping again. From behind, it looked as if it was too heavy for her, and that, at any moment, she was about to stumble.

She went into one of the apartment blocks at the far end, on the left. Each building had an entrance with a sign: STAIRCASE A. STAIRCASE B. STAIRCASE C. STAIRCASE D. Hers was Staircase A. I stayed outside for a while, waiting for a light to come on in a window. But I waited in vain. I wondered if there was a lift. I pictured her climbing Staircase A, clasping the cans. That image wouldn't fade, even in the metro on the way back.

ON SEVERAL OTHER evenings, I retraced my steps. I waited on a bench at Châtelet at exactly the same time as I had first come across her. I was on the lookout for the yellow coat.

The barrier opens as the train leaves and the tide of passengers pours onto the platform. When the next train arrives, they'll pile into the carriages. The platform empties, it fills again, and you let yourself drift off. With all the comings and goings, you no longer focus on anything precise, not even a yellow coat. A groundswell pushes you into one of the carriages.

I remember that, back then, the same poster was in every station. A couple with three fair-haired children all sitting round a table in an alpine chalet in the evening.

Their faces were illuminated by a lamp. Outside, it was snowing. It must have been Christmas. Written on top of the poster were the words: PUPIER, THE CHOCOLATE FOR FAMILIES.

The first week, I went to Vincennes once. The following week, twice. Then twice more. There were always too many people in the café at around seven in the evening for anyone to notice me. The second time, I ventured to ask the chubby blond barman if the woman in the yellow coat would come today. He frowned without seeming to understand. Someone from another table called him over. I don't think he heard me. But he wouldn't have had time to reply. It was peak hour for him, too. Perhaps she wasn't a regular at this café at all, and didn't live in this neighbourhood. Perhaps the person she had called from the phone box lived in the brick apartment block and, that particular evening, she had been visiting and had brought cans of food. Later, she had taken the metro in the other direction, as I had also done, and she had gone home, and I would never know precisely where. My only point of reference was Staircase A. But I would have to knock on each door on each landing and ask whoever was prepared to answer whether they knew a woman, about fifty years old, with a yellow coat and a scar on her face. Yes, well, she had been there one evening the week before, after buying cans of food and a packet of coffee from the grocery store on the street. What could they possibly say to me? That I had dreamed it all up?

And yet, there she was again in the fifth week. Just as I was coming out of the entrance to the metro, I saw her in the phone box. She was wearing her yellow coat. I wondered whether she, too, had just left the station. So she might have regular commutes and timetables in her life…I had trouble imagining her holding down a day job, like everyone else on the metro at that hour. Châtelet station. It was a vague starting point for further clues. Tens of thousands of people wind up at Châtelet before scattering to all points of the compass. Their paths mingle and blur, once and for all. There are fixed points in this tide of people. I should not have been content to wait on one of the station benches. I should have spent time hanging around the ticket offices and newspaper stands, in the long corridor with the escalator, and also in the other corridors. People can be there all day, but you only notice them after they've become a predictable feature of the place. Homeless people. Buskers. Pickpockets. People who have lost their way and who will never go up to the outside world again. Perhaps she never left Châtelet all day, either.

I was observing her in the phone box. It was like the first time: she didn't seem to have got through straightaway. She dialled the number again. She was speaking now, but the call was much shorter than the other evening. She hung up abruptly. She came out of the phone box and didn't stop at the café. She continued along Avenue de Paris, still with the gait of a dancer, until we reached the Château de Vincennes metro. Why didn't she get off at this stop, the end of the line? Because of the phone box and the café where she drank her customary kir before going home? And those other evenings when I hadn't seen her? Of course: she must have got off at Château de Vincennes.

I had to speak to her, or she would end up noticing that someone was following her. I tried to think of the words. The fewest possible. I would extend my hand. 'You used to call me Little Jewel. You must remember,' I would say to her. We were approaching the apartment block and, as on the first evening, I couldn't find it in me to address her. On the contrary, I let her draw further away. My legs felt heavy; I was filled with inertia. But also a sort of relief as her figure receded. That evening, she didn't stop in the grocery store to buy cans of food. She crossed the courtyard of the apartment block, and I stayed behind the metal gate. The courtyard was lit by a single globe above the entrance to Staircase A. In that light, the coat took on its yellow hue again. She looked exhausted as she trudged, hunching slightly, towards the staircase. At that moment, the title of a picture book I used to read, when my name was Little Jewel, came back to me: *The Old Circus Horse.*

When she had disappeared, I went through the metal gate. On the left was a glass door with a sign stuck on it—a list of names in alphabetical order and, next to each name, the corresponding staircase. A light was on behind the glass. I knocked. In the half-open door the face of a woman appeared, a brunette, short hair, quite young. I told her that I was looking for a lady who lived there. A lady who was single and wore a yellow coat.

Instead of shutting the door, the woman frowned, as if she was trying to remember a name.

'That must be Madame Boré. Staircase A...I've forgotten which floor.'

She ran her finger down the list. She pointed to a name. Boré. Staircase A. Fourth floor. I began to cross the courtyard. When I heard the concierge shutting her door, I did an about-turn and slipped out onto the street.

*

That evening, during the trip home on the metro, I kept thinking about the name. Boré. Yes, it was similar to the name of the man I had understood to be my mother's brother, Jean Borand. On Thursdays, he used to take me to his garage. Was it just a coincidence? And yet my mother's surname, as it appeared on my birth certificate, was Cardères. And O'Dauyé was the surname she had adopted as a sort of stage name. That was around the time when my own name was Little Jewel…

In my bedroom, I looked at the photos once again. I opened the diary and the address book that I kept packed away in the old biscuit tin and, in the middle of the diary, I came across a piece of paper torn out of a school exercise book—I recognised that scrap only too well. The tiny handwriting in blue ink did not belong to my mother. At the top of the page were the words: SONIA CARDÈRES. Under the name was a dash, then the following lines, which ran into the margin.

> *A missed opportunity. Unhappy in September. A quarrel with a blonde woman. Tendency to rely on dangerously easy solutions. What is lost will never be found. Falling for a non-Frenchman. A change in the months to come.*

Be careful at the end of July. A visit from a stranger. No danger, but exercise caution all the same. The journey will end well.

She had been to see a fortune teller or a palm reader. I assume she was uncertain about her future. *Tendency to rely on dangerously easy solutions.* All of a sudden, she had become frightened, like being on the scenic railway ride at an amusement park. It's too late to get off. It speeds up and soon you're wondering if the carriages will fly off the tracks. She could sense that everything was about to come tumbling down.

Unhappy in September. That was probably the summer when, out of the blue, I found myself alone in the country. The train was packed. I was wearing a label around my neck with an address written on it. *What is lost will never be found.* In the country, not long after, I received a postcard. It's in the bottom of the biscuit tin. Casablanca. La Place de France. 'Lots of love.' Not even a signature. Large handwriting, the same as in the diary and the address book. In the past, girls of my mother's age were taught to write in large script. *Falling for a non-Frenchman*—but which one? Several names that are not French feature in the address book. *Be careful at the end of July.* That was the month I was sent off to the country, to Fossombronne-la-Forêt. The painting by Tola Soungouroff was hanging on the wall of my bedroom so that, every morning when I woke up, my mother's eyes were staring at me. After receiving the post-card, I never heard another thing. All that was left was that gaze in the morning, and at night when I was in bed reading, or when I was sick. After a while, it dawned on me that she was staring not at me but into space.

No danger, but exercise caution all the same. The journey will end well. Words you repeat to yourself in the dark for reassurance. The day she went to see the clairvoyant, she probably knew that she was bound to leave for Morocco. And, anyway, it was there in the cards or in the lines of her hand. A journey. She left after I did: she was the one who took me to the Gare d'Austerlitz. I remember driving there, along the Seine. The station was next to the river. Many years later, I noticed that, if I happened to be near the Gare d'Austerlitz, I experienced an odd sensation. Everything suddenly felt colder and darker.

I had no idea where the painting could possibly be. Had they left it in my old room in Fossombronne-la-Forêt? Or else, after all this time, had it turned up, as I'd imagined, in some flea market on the outskirts of Paris? She had written the details of the painter, Tola Soungouroff, in her address book. It was the first name under S. The colour of the ink was different from the other names, the writing was smaller, as if she had wanted to make an effort. I presume Tola Soungouroff was one of the first people she met in Paris. One evening during her childhood, she had arrived at the Gare d'Austerlitz: I was almost certain about that. *The journey will end well.* I think the fortune teller made a mistake, but perhaps she disguised some of the truth so that her customers wouldn't be disheartened.

I would have liked to know what my mother was wearing that day at the Gare d'Austerlitz when she arrived in Paris. Not the yellow coat. And I wished I hadn't lost the picture book called *The Old Circus Horse*. It was given to me in the country, at Fossombronne-la-Forêt. No, that's wrong: I think I already had it in the apartment in Paris. And the painting was also hanging on the wall of one of the rooms in that apartment, the huge room with the three steps covered in white plush. The cover of the book featured a black horse. It was doing a lap, it looked like its last, its head bowed; it seemed exhausted, as if about to collapse. Yes, when I saw her crossing the courtyard of the apartment block, the image of the black horse came back to me. The horse was walking around the track and the harness seemed like a huge weight for it to bear. The harness was the same colour as the coat. Yellow.

SOMETIME BEFORE THE evening when I thought I recognised my mother in the metro, I had met a person called Moreau or Badmaev at the Mattei bookshop on Boulevard de Clichy. It stayed open late. I was looking for a detective novel. At midnight, we were the only customers, and he recommended a title on the Noir list. Then we talked as we walked together along the median strip down the boulevard. Occasionally, his voice had an odd intonation that made me think he was a foreigner. Later, he explained that Badmaev was the name of his father, whom he had hardly known. A Russian. But his mother was French. At that first meeting, he wrote his address on a piece of paper, under the name Moreau-Badmaev.

We chatted about this and that. He didn't tell me

much about himself that night, except that he lived near the Porte d'Orléans and that he was only in the neighbourhood by accident. A lucky accident, he said, because he had met me. He wanted to know if I read anything besides detective novels. I accompanied him to the Pigalle metro station. He asked me if we could see each other again. And he said, with a smile, 'That way, we'll get to see things more clearly.'

Those words made a strong impression on me. It was as if he had read my thoughts. Yes. I had reached a time in my life when I wanted to see things more clearly.

Everything seemed so confusing from the beginning, from my earliest childhood memories…Sometimes, the memories appeared around five in the morning, at that dangerous time when you can't get back to sleep. So I waited before going out, to make sure the first cafés would be open. I knew perfectly well that, as soon as I stepped outside, the memories would dissolve like remnants of a bad dream. It's the same all year round. On winter mornings when it's dark and the air is crisp, the lights are still shining and the first customers are gathered at the counter like conspirators. They give you the illusion that the day will be a new adventure. And that illusion stays with you for at least some of the morning. In summer, when it's hot first thing and there's no traffic, I was always sitting on the terrace of whichever café was already open, and I imagined that all I'd have to do would be to head down Rue Blanche and I would come out at the beach. On those mornings, too, the bad memories dissolved.

The Moreau-Badmaev fellow had arranged for us to meet in a café called Le Corentin, near the Porte d'Orléans. I arrived first. It was seven in the evening and already dark. He'd told me that he couldn't get there any earlier because he worked in an office. A tall brown-haired fellow came in, about twenty-five, wearing a leather jacket. He spotted me immediately and sat down opposite. I'd been worried that he might not recognise me. He would never know that I was once called Little Jewel. Who still knew, apart from me? And my mother? Perhaps I should tell him, one of these days. In order to try to see things more clearly.

He smiled, and said that he had been worried about missing our meeting. That evening, he had been held up at work later than usual. He told me that his shifts changed from week to week. For now, he was working during the day, but the following week it would be from ten in the evening until seven in the morning. I asked him what his job was. He told me that he tuned into radio broadcasts in foreign languages and wrote up translations and summaries. It was for an organisation, but I didn't really grasp whether it was connected to a news service or some branch of government. He had got the job because he knew twenty-odd languages. I was very impressed, especially as I only spoke French. But he said it wasn't that difficult. Once you've learned two or three languages, you just need to maintain the momentum. Anyone could do it. And so, what did I do? he asked. Well, at the moment, I survived on occasional part-time jobs, but I still hoped to settle on something. I felt the need of a regular job—especially for my morale.

He leaned over me and lowered his voice. 'Why? Are you feeling depressed?'

I wasn't shocked by his question. I hardly knew him, but I felt at ease with him.

'What exactly are you looking for in life?' He seemed apologetic about asking such an abstract and earnest question. He stared at me with his bright eyes. I noticed that they were blue-grey. He also had beautiful hands.

'What I am looking for in life...' I took a deep breath. I absolutely had to say something. Someone like him, who spoke twenty languages, would not have understood if I said nothing.

'I'm looking for...a human connection...'

He didn't seem disappointed by my answer. Again, he stared at me with his bright, clear gaze; I had to lower my eyes. And those beautiful hands, flat on the table—I could imagine those fine, long fingers sliding over the keys of a piano. I was so susceptible to eyes and hands.

He said, 'I was struck by a word you used earlier: "settle".'

I didn't recall using the word. But I was flattered that he had found such significance in the few words I had said. Such banal words.

'The problem is settling on something…'

At that moment, despite his calm, gentle voice, he seemed as anxious as I was. He even asked if I had ever felt that horrible sensation of floating, as if a current were sweeping you away and there was nothing to hang on to.

Yes, I knew that feeling. Days and days went by, indistinguishable one from another, sliding as evenly as the moving walkway at Châtelet. I was swept along an endless corridor; I didn't even need to walk. And yet, one evening soon, out of nowhere, a yellow coat would catch my eye. In that crowd of strangers, one of whom I had become, a single colour would stand out, a colour that I could not lose sight of if I wanted to know a bit more about myself.

'We have to settle on something so that life is no longer this constant floating.' He smiled at me as if he wanted to sound less serious. 'Once we find it, then everything will be fine, don't you think?'

I had the impression that he was trying to remember my first name. Once again, I had the urge to introduce myself by saying, 'I used to be called Little Jewel.' I would then tell him everything, from the beginning. But all I said was, 'My first name is Thérèse.'

The other night, on the median strip, I had asked him what his first name was and he had replied, 'No first name. Just call me Badmaev. Or Moreau, if you prefer.' I was taken aback. But later I thought it was his way of protecting himself, of keeping his distance. He didn't want to get too close to people. Perhaps he was hiding something.

He suggested that I come back to his place. He had a book to lend me. He lived in one of the apartment blocks opposite Le Corentin café, on the other side of Boulevard Jourdan. Brick apartment blocks, like the one in Vincennes where I would see my mother crossing the courtyard. We walked past a series of identical façades. At number 11 Rue Monticelli, we climbed a set of stairs to the fourth floor. The door opened onto a hallway with dark-red linoleum. At the end of the hallway was his bedroom. There was a mattress on the floor and books piled along the walls. He asked if I'd like to sit on the only chair, in front of the window.

'Before I forget—I have to give you this book.'

He bent over the stacks of books and appraised each one. Finally, he picked a book that stuck out from the others because of its red cover. He held it out to me. I opened it at the title page: *On the Outer Limits of Life.*

He seemed apologetic, and said, 'If you find it boring, you don't have to read it.'

He sat on the edge of the mattress. The room was lit only by a small bare bulb attached to the top of a tripod. The light was weak. Next to the mattress, instead of a table, was a gigantic radio with fabric over the speaker. I had seen a similar one at Fossombronne-la-Forêt. He caught me looking at it.

'I really like this radio,' he said. 'I sometimes use it for my work. When I can work from home.'

He leaned over and turned a knob. A green light came on. A muffled voice began speaking in a foreign language.

'Do you want to know how I work?' He picked up a writing pad and a biro from the top of the radio and wrote, on and off, while listening to the voice. 'It's easy…I take it all down in shorthand.'

He came over and handed me a page. I have kept the piece of paper with me ever since that evening.

Just below the shorthand were these words: *Niet lang geleden slaagden matrozen er in de sirenen, enkele mijlen zuidelijd van de azoren, te vangen.*

And then the translation: 'Not so long ago, sailors managed to capture mermaids, a few miles south of the Azores.'

'It's in Dutch. But he read it with a slight Flemish accent from Anvers.'

He turned the knob and the voice faded. He left the green light on. So that was his work. He was given a list of programs to listen to, either during the day or at night, and he had to translate them before the next day.

'Sometimes they're programs from a long way away… people speaking odd languages.'

He listened to them at night, in his room, to keep in practice. I pictured him lying on his bed, in the darkness punctured by the greenish light.

He sat down on the mattress again. He told me that, since he'd been in the apartment, he'd hardly ever used the kitchen. There was another bedroom but he left it empty and never went in there. Besides, after listening to so many foreign broadcasts, he ended up not really knowing what country he was in.

The window looked onto a large courtyard and the façades of apartment blocks where, on every floor, the lights were on in other windows. Sometime later, when I followed my mother home for the first time, I was sure that the view from her window was the same as the one from Moreau-Badmaev's window. I looked in the street directory hoping to find her name, and I was surprised at how many people lived there. Fifty or so, among whom were at least ten single women. But her maiden name was not listed, nor was the assumed name that she had used in the past. The concierge had not yet told me that her name was Boré. And then I had to look up the street directory again. I had lost Moreau-Badmaev's telephone number. There were just as many names listed under his street as my mother's. Yes, apartment blocks, whether at Vincennes or at the Porte d'Orléans, were identical. His name, Moreau-Badmaev, was there. It was proof that I had not dreamed it all up.

That evening, while I was looking out the window, he said that the view was 'a bit dreary'. Early on, he'd felt stifled here. He could hear every sound from his neighbours, the ones on his floor and the ones living above and below. It was a constant racket, like the noise in a prison. He thought he was destined to be locked in a cell in the middle of hundreds and hundreds of cells occupied by families or single people like himself. At the time, he was just back from a trip to Iran and had lost the habit of living in Paris, in big cities. He had gone there to learn a language, Persian of the plains.

It was not taught anywhere, not even at the School of Oriental Languages. So he'd gone there the year before to learn it on the spot. Coming back to Paris, to the Porte d'Orléans, had been difficult, but now the noise of the other tenants didn't bother him at all. All he had to do was switch on the radio and gently turn the dial. And, once again, he would be far away. He didn't need to travel. All he needed was to turn on the green light.

'If you like, I could teach you Persian of the plains…'

He said it jokingly, but the sentence resonated because of the word 'plains'. I knew I would be leaving Paris soon and had no real reason to feel trapped by anything. All sorts of horizons stretched out before me into the distance, plains as far as the eye could see, sloping down to the ocean. One last time, I wanted to assemble a few meagre memories, find some vestiges of my childhood, just like the traveller who keeps an out-of-date identity card in his pocket until the end. There wasn't much to gather together before leaving.

It was nine o'clock in the evening. I told him I had to go home. He said that, next time, if it suited me, he would invite me for dinner. And he would give me a lesson in Persian of the plains.

He walked with me to the metro. I didn't recognise the Porte d'Orléans, and yet, until I was sixteen, it was where I used to arrive every time I came to Paris. Back then, the bus I took from Fossombronne-la-Forêt stopped in front of La Rotonde café.

He was still speaking to me about Persian of the plains. It was like Finnish, he said. It was also a pleasant language to listen to. You could hear the rustle of wind in the grasses and the murmur of waterfalls.

IN THE BEGINNING, I was aware of a funny smell on the stairs. It came from the red carpet, which must have been decomposing. You could already see the wooden steps coming through in a few spots. So many people had climbed up and down these stairs, back when this building was a hotel...The staircase was steep and led directly from the covered entrance on the street. I knew my mother had lived in this hotel: the address was on my birth certificate. One day, when I was looking through the classifieds to find a room to rent, I was surprised to come across the address under the heading STUDIO RENTALS.

I turned up at the appointed time. A man of about fifty with a ruddy complexion was waiting for me on the pavement. He took me up to the first floor and showed me a bedroom with a little bathroom. He insisted I pay three months' rent in cash. Fortunately, I still had enough money on me. He took me to a café, on the corner of Boulevard de Clichy, to fill in and sign the papers. He explained to me that the hotel had been closed down and that the rooms had become studios.

'My mother lived in this hotel...'

I heard myself say the sentence slowly and was startled. What had got into me?

'Oh, really?' he said distractedly. 'Your mother?' He was of an age to have known her. I asked if he had been in charge of the hotel in the past. No. He had bought it last year with some business partners and they had done various renovations.

'You know,' he said, 'it wasn't such a glamorous hotel.'

On my first night there, I imagined that perhaps my mother had lived in the room I was in. Things had suddenly fallen into place on the evening I was looking for a room to rent, when I saw the address in the newspaper: 11 Rue Coustou. For a little while before then, I would open the old biscuit tin, flick through the diary and address book, look at the photos...But I confess that I had never previously opened the tin, or else, if I did open it, I never had the urge to focus on what seemed to be nothing more than old scraps of paper. Ever since I was a child, I'd kept this tin with me; like Tola Soungouroff's painting, it had always been part of the furniture and accompanied me everywhere. I even stored some cheap jewellery in there, the sort of trinkets you keep for ages and don't pay much attention to. And, if you happen to lose them, you realise that you were never aware of certain details about them. So I didn't remember what the frame of Soungouroff's painting looked like. And if I had lost the biscuit tin, I would have forgotten that on the lid there was a torn sticker on which you could still read: LEFÈVRE-UTILE. One has to beware of so-called witnesses.

I had come back to the beginning, since that address was on my birth certificate as my mother's place of residence. And I had probably lived there, too, early in my life. One evening, when Moreau-Badmaev was walking me home, I told him my story and he said, 'So, you've found your old family home.'

And we both burst out laughing. The entrance is concealed by honeysuckle; the gate has stayed shut for so long that weeds have grown on the other side and you can only open it a bit to squeeze through. In the depths of the plain, under the light of the moon, was the castle of our childhood. With a candelabra in our hand, we walk through the blue living room and the picture gallery lined with portraits of our ancestors. Nothing has changed; everything has stayed in exactly the same spot, under a layer of dust. We climb up the main staircase. At the end of the corridor, we finally arrive at the children's bedroom.

Moreau-Badmaev was having a laugh, describing my return to the family estate as it might have happened in another life. But the window of my bedroom looked out onto Rue Puget, a short street, much narrower than Rue Coustou and making a sort of triangle with it. My bedroom was at the apex of the triangle. There were no shutters or curtains. At night, the illuminated sign on the garage further down Rue Coustou flashed red and green on the wall above my bed. It didn't worry me. On the contrary, I found it comforting. Someone was watching over me. Perhaps the red and green flashes dated back a long time, to when my mother and I were in the bedroom, lying on the same bed, trying to get to sleep, as I was now. The lights went on and off, on and off, and I found it soothing as I slipped off to sleep. Why had I rented this room, when I could have chosen one in another neighbourhood? But it wouldn't have had red and green flashes, as regular as heartbeats, which I ended up telling myself were the only traces left of the past.

EACH DAY I had to go over to the Bois de Boulogne district, to the home of some rich people whose daughter I looked after. I'd landed the job one afternoon when, as a last resort, I fronted up at the Taylor Agency, an employment agency that I chose at random from the pages of a telephone directory.

A red-headed man with a moustache and wearing a glen plaid suit showed me into a dark-panelled office. He told me to take a seat. I found the courage to tell him that it was the first time I'd tried out for this sort of job.

'Don't you want to continue with your studies?'

His question took me aback. I told him I wasn't enrolled in any course.

'When I saw you come in, I assumed you were a student.'

He pronounced the word with such respect that I wondered what wonderful things it evoked for him and I was truly sorry that I wasn't a student.

'I might have a job for you—three hours a day—a babysitting job.'

I immediately had the impression that no one ever made an appointment at the Taylor Agency and that this red-headed man spent long, lonely afternoons sitting at his desk, daydreaming about female students. On one of the walls, to my left, was a large sign on which were precisely drawn pictures of men dressed as maître d's and as chauffeurs, and of women in what looked like nannies' and nurses' uniforms. On the bottom of the sign, written in large black letters: THE ANDRÉ TAYLOR AGENCY.

He smiled at me. He told me that the sign was from his father's era and that I would certainly not need to wear a uniform. The people who were to interview me lived near Neuilly and were looking for someone to take care of their little girl each afternoon.

The first time I went to their place, it was a rainy day in November. I hadn't slept the night before and I wondered what they would think of me. The man at the agency had said they were quite young, and he'd given me a piece of paper with their name and address: Valadier, 70 Boulevard Maurice-Barrès. It had been raining all morning; it made me want to leave my room, leave Paris. As soon as I had a bit of money, I would head for the Midi, or even further, down south. I tried to hang on to this plan, and not let myself sink into despair. I had to tread water, be patient. The only reason I contacted the Taylor Agency was as a last-ditch effort to persevere. Otherwise, I would never have had the courage to leave my room or my bed.

I could still picture the sign on the wall of the agency. The red-headed man would have been shocked if I had told him that I would not have minded wearing a nanny's uniform or, especially, a nurse's uniform. A uniform would have helped me to summon my courage and my endurance, the way a corset helps you to walk with an upright posture. In any case, I had no choice. Until then, I'd only been lucky enough to find two temporary jobs as a salesgirl, first at the department store Les Trois Quartiers, and then in a perfume shop on the Grands Boulevards. The Taylor Agency might find me a more secure job. But I had no illusions about my chances. I was not a performer like my mother had been. When I lived in Fossombronne-la-Forêt, I used to work at the Auberge Verte on the Grande-Rue. A lot of customers frequented this hotel, often people from Paris. My work was not very demanding: I was either at the bar, or in the dining room, or sometimes at reception. Every evening in winter, I used to light the fire in the little wood-panelled room near the bar, where you could read the papers or play cards. I worked there until I was sixteen.

The rain had stopped by the time I entered the metro at Place Blanche. I got out at Porte Maillot and was filled with dread. I knew this neighbourhood. I told myself that I must have dreamed about visiting these people for the first time. So now I was living what I had dreamed: the metro and the walk to their house, and that was why I had the sensation of déjà vu. Boulevard Maurice-Barrès ran alongside the Bois de Boulogne and, as I continued walking, the sensation grew stronger and stronger until I became alarmed. But then I wondered if I wasn't in fact dreaming. I pinched my arm, I hit my forehead with the palm of my hand in an effort to wake up. Sometimes I knew I was in a dream, that I was in danger, but that none of it was really serious because I could wake myself up at any moment. One night, I'd been condemned to death—it was in England and I was to be hanged the following morning—and they'd taken me to my cell, but I was completely calm, I smiled at them,

I knew I was going to give them the slip and wake up in the bedroom on Rue Coustou.

I had to go through a metal gate and down a gravel path. I rang the doorbell at number 70, which looked like a mansion. A blonde woman greeted me and told me that her name was Madame Valadier. She seemed embarrassed to say 'madame', as if the word didn't apply to her but she was obliged by circumstances to use it. Later, when the fellow from the Taylor Agency asked me, 'So, how did you find Monsieur and Madame Valadier?' I said, 'They're a nice couple.' He seemed surprised by my response.

They were both about thirty-five. He was tall, dark-haired, with a gentle voice, and quite elegant; his wife was ash-blonde. They sat next to each other on the couch, as self-conscious as I was. It was as if they were camping out in the huge living room on the first floor where—apart from the couch and an armchair—there was not a stick of furniture. Nor were there any paintings on the white walls.

That afternoon, the little girl and I went for a short walk on the other side of the avenue, along the paths near the Jardin d'Acclimatation amusement park. She was silent the whole time, but she seemed to trust me, as if this were not the first time we had gone walking together. I, too, had the feeling that I knew her well and that we had been down these paths together before.

Back at the house, she wanted to show me her bedroom, a large room on the second floor that looked out over the trees of the Jardin d'Acclimatation. From the wood panelling and the two built-in glass cabinets on either side of the fireplace, I assumed that it had once been a living room or a study, but never a child's bedroom. Her bed wasn't a child's bed, either, but was broad with upholstered surrounds. Ivory chess pieces were displayed in one of the glass cabinets. No doubt the upholstered bed and the chess pieces were in the house when the Valadiers moved in, along with other items the previous tenants had forgotten or didn't have time to pack up.

The little girl did not take her eyes off me. Perhaps she wanted to know what I thought. Finally, I said, 'You've got plenty of room here,' and she nodded without much conviction. Her mother came in. She said they'd only been living in the house for a few months, but she didn't say where they'd been before that. The little girl went to a school close by, in Rue de la Ferme, and I was to collect her every afternoon at half past four. I must have said, 'Yes, Madame.' At once, a wry smile lit up her face. 'Don't call me Madame. Call me...Véra.' She hesitated, as if she had invented the name. Earlier, when she greeted me, I had taken her to be English or American; I now realised she had a Parisian accent, one that, in old novels, is described as working class.

'Véra is a very nice name,' I said.

'Do you think so?'

She switched on the lamp on the bedside table and said, 'There's not enough light in this room.'

The little girl, lying on the parquet floor, at the base of one of the cabinets, was leaning on her elbows and solemnly turning the pages of a school exercise book.

'It's not very convenient,' she explained. 'We need to find her a study so she can do her homework.'

I had the same impression as I had earlier, when they talked to me in the living room: the Valadiers were camping out in this house.

She clearly noticed my surprise, because she continued, 'I don't know whether we'll be staying here for long. As a matter of fact, my husband doesn't like the furniture.'

She offered that wry smile again and asked where I lived. I told her that I had found a room in what had once been a hotel.

'Oh yes...we lived in a hotel, too, for a long time.'

She wanted to know what area I lived in.

'Near Place Blanche.'

'Oh, that's where I grew up,' she said, with a slight frown. 'I lived on Rue de Douai.'

At that instant, she resembled one of those aloof, blonde American women who star in thrillers; I thought her voice was dubbed—exactly like being at the cinema—and was surprised to hear her speaking French.

'On my way home from the Lycée Jules-Ferry, I used to walk around the block and go through Place Blanche.' She hadn't been back to the neighbourhood for a long time. For many years, she had lived in London. That's where she had met her husband.

The little girl was no longer taking any notice of us. She was still lying on the floor, writing in a different exercise book, without faltering, completely absorbed by her task. 'She's doing her homework,' said Madame Valadier. 'You'll see…at seven, her handwriting is almost that of an adult.'

It was dark, and yet it was barely five o'clock. Silence everywhere, the same silence I had known at Fossombronne-la-Forêt, at the same time of day and at the same age as the little girl. I suspect that, at that age, I, too, had an adult's handwriting. I got into trouble because I stopped using a fountain pen, and wrote with a ballpoint instead. Out of curiosity, I checked what the little girl was using: a ballpoint. At her school, in Rue de la Ferme, they probably allowed students to use Bic pens with transparent tips and black, red or green lids. Did she know how to do capital letters? In any case, I doubted they still taught edged-pen lettering.

They took me back to the ground floor. On the left, a double door opened onto a large empty room, at the end of which was a desk. Monsieur Valadier was sitting on the corner of the desk, talking on the telephone. A chandelier cast a harsh light over him. He was speaking in a strange-sounding language that only Moreau-Badmaev could have understood: perhaps Persian of the plains. A cigarette was stuck in the corner of his mouth. He waved to me.

'Say hello to the Moulin Rouge for me,' Madame Valadier whispered, staring at me with a sad look as if she envied me going back to that neighbourhood.

'Goodbye, Madame.'

It had slipped out but still she corrected me. 'No. Goodbye, Véra.'

So I repeated it: 'Goodbye, Véra.' Was that actually her name or had she chosen it, one day at Lycée Jules-Ferry when she was feeling sad, because she didn't like her real name?

She proceeded towards the door with the lithe gait of aloof, unfathomable blonde women.

'Walk with mademoiselle for a bit,' she said to her daughter. 'There's a good girl.'

The little girl nodded and gave me an anxious look.

'I often send her round the block at night. She likes it. It makes her feel like a big girl. The other evening she even wanted to do a second trip...She wants to practise so she's not frightened anymore.'

From behind us, at the end of the room, the gentle voice of Monsieur Valadier reached me, in between long stretches of silence and, each time, I wondered if his telephone conversation had come to an end.

'Soon, you won't be frightened of the dark anymore, and we won't have to leave the light on so you can go to sleep.'

Madame Valadier opened the front door. When I saw that the little girl was about to go outside wearing only her skirt and blouse, I said, 'Perhaps you should put on a coat.'

She seemed surprised and almost reassured that I might give her advice, and she turned to her mother.

'Yes, yes...Go and put on your coat.'

She ran up the stairs. Madame Valadier looked at me intently with her clear, pale eyes.

'Thank you,' she said. 'You'll know how to look after her...We are sometimes so lost, my husband and I...'

She was still staring at me with a look that made me think she was about to cry. And yet her face remained impassive and there was not the slightest trace of a tear.

*

We had gone further than around the block. I said to the little girl, 'Perhaps you should go back home now.'

But she wanted to keep walking with me. I explained that I had to go and catch the metro.

As we went along the avenue, it felt as if I had been here before. The smell of the dead leaves and the damp earth reminded me of something. It was the same feeling I'd had in the little girl's bedroom. Everything I had wanted to forget up until now or, rather, everything I had avoided thinking about, like someone with vertigo trying not to look down, all of it was going to emerge bit by bit, and now I was ready to face up to it. We were walking down the path that runs along the Jardin d'Acclimatation, and the little girl took my hand to cross the avenue in the direction of the Porte Maillot.

'Do you live far away?'

She asked the question as if she hoped that I'd take her home with me. We had reached the entrance of the metro. I was convinced that if I just said the word she would follow me down the steps and never return to her parents. I knew exactly how she felt. It even seemed as if that was how it was meant to be.

'Now it's my turn to walk you home.'

She seemed crestfallen at the prospect. But I told her that next week I would take her for a trip in the metro. We were walking back along the path. It was two or three weeks after I thought I had recognised my mother in the corridors of Châtelet station. I imagined her at this time of day, crossing the courtyard of the apartment block, on the other side of Paris, wearing her yellow coat. On the stairs, she would stop on each landing. *A missed opportunity. What is lost will never be found.* Perhaps in twenty years' time, the little girl, like me, would find her parents again, one evening at peak hour, in those same corridors where the train connections were signposted.

There was a light on in one of the French windows on the ground floor, in the room where Monsieur Valadier had been on the telephone. I rang the bell, but no one came. The little girl was quiet, as if she was used to this sort of situation. After a while, she said, 'They've gone,' and she smiled and shrugged. I considered taking her back to my place to spend the night. She must have read my mind. 'Yes…I'm sure they've gone.' She wanted to persuade me that we had no further reason to stay here, but, just to be sure, I went up to the lighted window and peered in. The room was empty. I rang the doorbell again. Finally, someone was coming. The instant the door opened a crack, in a ray of light, I saw the little girl's face fill with awful disappointment. It was her father. He was wearing a coat.

'Have you been here for long?' he asked in a tone of polite indifference. 'Do you want to come in?'

He spoke to us as if we were visitors who had called by unannounced.

He leaned over to the little girl. 'So, did you have a nice long walk?'

She didn't answer.

'My wife has left to have dinner with some friends,' he said, 'and I was just about to join her.'

The little girl hesitated before going inside. She looked at me one last time and said, 'See you tomorrow,' her tone apprehensive, as if she wasn't sure whether I'd come back. Monsieur Valadier was smiling vaguely. Then the door shut behind them.

I stood, not moving, on the other side of the boulevard, under the trees. On the second floor, a light went on in the window of the little girl's room. Soon, I saw Monsieur Valadier hurry out of the house. He got into a black car. She must have been alone in the house and left a light on so she could go to sleep. I thought of how lucky we'd been: a little later, and no one would have come to open the door.

ON THE FOLLOWING Sunday—or the Sunday after that—I went back to Vincennes. I wanted to go earlier than I had the other times, before nightfall. This time I got out at the end of the line, at Château de Vincennes. It was sunny that autumn Sunday and, once again, as I wandered past the château and turned into Rue du Quartier-de-Cavalerie, I felt as if I was in a provincial town. I was the only person out walking, and at the top of the street, behind a wall, I heard the clopping of horses' hooves.

I slipped into a daydream about what might have been: after many years away, I had just got off the train at a little station in my 'home country'. I can't remember which book it was where I first came across the expression 'home country'. Those two words must have connected with something that affected me deeply or else stirred up a memory. After all, in my childhood, I had also known a country railway station, where I used to arrive from Paris, wearing that label around my neck, with my name written on it.

As soon as I caught sight of the apartment block at the end of the street, my dream vanished. There was no such thing as my home country, only an outlying suburb where no one was waiting for me.

I went through the gate and knocked on the concierge's lodge. She poked her head through the half-open door. She seemed to recognise me, even though we had only spoken once before. She was wearing a pink woollen dressing-gown.

'I wanted to ask you about Madame…Boré.'

I faltered over the name and feared she might not know who I was talking about. But this time she didn't need to consult the list of tenants stuck on the door.

'The woman on the fourth floor of A?'

'Yes.'

I'd made a point of remembering which floor. Since I'd discovered that it was the fourth, I often imagined her moving more and more slowly as she climbed the steps. One night, I even dreamed that she fell down the stairwell. When

I woke up, I couldn't tell if it was suicide or an accident. Or perhaps I had pushed her.

'You've been here before—the other day, wasn't it…'

'Yes.'

She smiled at me. I looked like someone she could trust.

'You know she's up to her old tricks again…' Her tone was indifferent, as if nothing about the woman on the fourth floor of A could surprise her. 'Are you family?'

I was afraid to say yes. And bring down the ancient curse on myself, the stigma from back then.

'No. Not at all.'

In the nick of time, I had avoided being sucked into the slime.

'I know some of her family,' I said. 'They sent me to find out how she is…'

'What do you want me to tell you? Nothing has changed, you know.' She shrugged. 'She won't even talk to me anymore. Or else she'll have a go at me for no reason.'

I was not surprised by anything she said. Now, even after all these years, a vision rose before me, as if it had emerged from the deep: the grimacing face, the dilated eyes, and something like spittle on those lips. And the screeching voice, and the stream of abuse. Anyone who didn't know her would not have been able to imagine the abrupt transformation of such a beautiful face. I could feel myself in the grip of fear again.

'Have you come to visit her?'

'No.'

'You need to tell her family that she isn't paying her rent anymore.'

Those words, and perhaps also the neighbourhood where I went to pick up the little girl every afternoon, made me think of the apartment near the Bois de Boulogne which, in spite of myself, I still remembered: the large room with three steps covered in plush; the painting by Tola Soungouroff; my bedroom, even more empty than the little girl's. How did she pay the rent back then?

'It will be tricky to kick her out. And, anyway, she's known around the neighbourhood. They've even given her a nickname...'

'What is it?' I was genuinely curious. Was it the same one she had twenty years ago?

'They call her Death Cheater.'

She said it kindly, as if it were a term of affection.

'Sometimes we think she's going to give up the ghost

and then the next day she's cheerful and charming, or else she does something really nasty.'

For me, the nickname had another meaning. I'd been under the impression that she'd died in Morocco and now I was discovering that she'd been resuscitated somewhere in the suburbs of Paris.

'Has she lived here long?' I asked.

'Oh, yes! She was here well before me. It must be more than six years now.'

So, she was living in this building while I was still at Fossombronne-la-Forêt. I recalled an overgrown vacant block that we called Kraut's Field, not far from the church. On Thursday afternoons, when there was no school, we used to explore the jungle there, or play hide-and-seek. The remains of a helmet and a mouldy pea coat had been found on the block—no doubt left by a soldier at the end of the war—and we were always afraid of coming across his skeleton. I didn't know what Kraut meant. Frédérique, the woman who knew my mother, and who had taken me into her home, wasn't there the day I asked her friend, the brunette with the boxer's face, what it meant. Perhaps she thought I was frightened by the word and wanted to reassure me. She smiled and told me that it was a name people used for the Germans, but that it wasn't really a rude word. 'And your mother was called the Kraut...It was a joke.'

Frédérique wasn't very happy that the brunette had told me this, but she didn't elaborate. She was my mother's friend—they must have known each other when my mother was 'a dancer'. Frédérique Chatillon was her full name. Her women friends were always at the house in Fossombronne-la-Forêt, even when she wasn't there: Rose-Marie, Jeannette, Madeleine-Louis, others whose names I've forgotten, and the brunette who had also known my mother when she was 'a dancer' and who didn't like her.

'Does she live alone?' I asked the concierge.

'For a long time, there was a man who used to visit her. He worked with horses somewhere around here. He looked North African.'

'Doesn't he come anymore?'

'Not for a while.'

Because of all my questions, she was starting to look at me somewhat suspiciously. I was tempted to tell her everything. My mother went to Paris when she was young. She was a dancer. They called her the Kraut. They called me Little Jewel. It was too long and complicated to explain right there, outside, in the courtyard of this apartment block.

'The problem is that she owes me two hundred francs...'

I always carried my money on me, in a little canvas pouch tied around my waist. I fossicked in the pouch. I still had a hundred-franc note, a fifty-franc note and some change. I held out the two notes and told her I would come back with the rest.

'Thank you very much.'

She slipped them into one of the pockets of her dressing-gown. Her wariness had vanished all of a sudden. I could have asked her any old question about Death Cheater.

'About the rent...I'll let you know when you come back.'

I hadn't really planned on coming back. What more would I learn? And what was the point?

'They've cut off her electricity a few times. And each time, I'm glad for her sake, because she uses an electric blanket—it's dangerous.'

I imagined her plugging the cord of her electric blanket into a socket. She'd always liked those sorts of devices, which seem so cutting edge for a while and then become obsolete, or else end up as everyday items. I remembered that, back in more prosperous times for her, when we lived in the big apartment near the Bois de Boulogne, someone brought her a box covered in green leather, which allowed us to listen to the radio. Later, I worked out that it must have been one of the first transistor radios.

'You should warn her not to use an electric blanket.'

Well, sorry, it was not as simple as that. Had she ever, in her whole life, heeded good advice? And, anyway, it was too late.

'You don't happen to know the name of the man who came to visit her?'

The concierge had kept a letter from him, which he sent three months ago with payment for the rent. Through the half-open door, I saw her rummaging among papers in a big box.

'I can't find it…Anyhow, I don't think that man will come by again.'

He was probably the one she was calling in the evenings from the phone box. After twelve years, by some miracle, there was still someone she could count on. But she had ended up scaring him away, too. Already, back when I was called Little Jewel, she could spend whole days in her room, cut off from the world, seeing no one, not even me, and, after a while, I had no idea whether she was still there, or if she had left me alone in that huge apartment.

'What's her place like?' I asked.

'Two small rooms and a kitchen with a shower.'

Her mattress was more than likely on the floor, next to the electricity socket. That way, it would be easier to turn on the electric blanket.

'You should go up and see her. It would be a surprise for her to have a visitor.'

If we found ourselves face to face, she wouldn't even know who I was. She had forgotten Little Jewel and all the hopes she had invested in me when she gave me that name. Unfortunately for her, I had not become a famous artist.

'Can you do me a favour?' The concierge rummaged in the big box again and held out an envelope. 'It's a reminder about her bills. I don't dare give it to her in person, or she'll swear at me again.'

I took the envelope and crossed the courtyard. As I stepped onto the entrance porch of Staircase A, I felt something pressing down inside my chest; I could scarcely breathe. It was one of those staircases with cement steps and a metal handrail, like in schools or hospitals. On each landing, bright, almost white light shone through a big window. I stopped on the first landing. There was a door on each side, and one in the middle, all made of the same dark wood, with the names of the tenants marked on them. I tried to get my breath back, but the feeling of constriction was getting worse and I was frightened I was going to suffocate. To calm myself down, I imagined what the name on her door would be. Her real one or her stage name? Or just: THE KRAUT or DEATH CHEATER. In the days when I was called Little Jewel and I would come home alone to our building near the Bois de Boulogne, I used to stay back in the lift for a long time. It had a black metal gate, and to enter you had to push two glass swing doors. Inside, there was a red velvet bench, glass panels on each side, and a neon globe in the ceiling. It was like a bedroom. My clearest memories are of the lift.

On the second landing, I felt the pressure stifling me again. So I tried to recall the other staircase, with its thick red carpet and copper banisters: on each floor there was only one large door with two panels. White.

I was seized by vertigo. I stepped away as far as I could from the handrail and flattened myself against the wall. But I was determined to climb the whole way. In the back of my mind was the voice of Madame Valadier—Véra—telling me about the little girl: 'I often send her round the block at night...She wants to practise so she's not frightened anymore.' Well, it was the same for me. I would continue on up, I would go right to Death Cheater's door, and I would ring the buzzer in bursts until she opened. And, just as the door opened, I would compose myself and say coolly, 'You shouldn't use an electric blanket. It's a really stupid thing to do.' And I'd watch dispassionately as her face grew pale and distorted with anger. I remembered that she was not keen on people talking to her about mundane details. But that was back when we were in the big apartment, when she wanted to remain mysterious.

I had reached the fourth floor. There were three doors there, too, but the dirty beige paintwork on the doors and walls was flaking off. A light bulb hung from the ceiling. A piece of graph paper was sticky-taped to the left-hand door. In black ink, in messy handwriting, was the word BORÉ.

Rather than climbing a staircase, the impression I had was of having descended into a well. It had taken twelve years for the white door with two panels to become this old flaking door, in the weak light of the bulb, and for the little gold plaque, engraved with the name COMTESSE SONIA O'DAUYÉ, to become nothing more than a scrap of paper from a schoolbook with that unprepossessing name scrawled across it: BORÉ.

I stood in front of the door, without ringing the buzzer. When I used to come home alone to the big apartment near the Bois de Boulogne and ring the buzzer, often no one answered. So I'd go down the staircase and telephone from a café not far along the avenue. The bar owner was kind to me, as were the customers. They seemed to know who I was. They must have found out. One day, one of them said, 'It's the little girl from 129.' I didn't have any money and they didn't make me pay for the call. I went into the booth. The phone was too high for me and I had to stand on tiptoes to dial the number: PASSY 15 28. But no one answered at the residence of Comtesse Sonia O'Dauyé.

For a second, I was tempted to ring. I was almost certain she would come to the door. First of all, the apartment was too small for the noise of the buzzer to fade away as it had in the succession of rooms at PASSY 15 28. And also her visitors were so few that she would be on the lookout for any break in her monotonous solitude. Or was she still hoping for a visit from that man who hadn't come for a while—the one who looked North African...But perhaps her periodic bouts of antisocial behaviour—when she'd lock herself in her room or disappear for several days—had got worse after twelve years.

I placed the envelope on the doormat. Then I scuttled down the stairs. At each landing, I felt lighter, as if I had dodged danger. In the courtyard, I was surprised to be able to breathe again. What a relief to be able to walk on firm ground, the security of the pavement... Just now, in front of that door, it would only have been a matter of a gesture, a step, and I would have been sucked down into the slime.

*

I had enough change left to take the metro. In the carriage, I dropped onto a seat. After the euphoria of fleeing the apartment block, I was now overwhelmed with exhaustion and despair. As much as I told myself that this woman they called Death Cheater no longer had anything at all to do with me, and wouldn't even recognise me if we happened to run into each other, I still couldn't banish my unease. I didn't get off at Nation, where I should have changed lines, but I was having trouble breathing again, so I left the metro and went up for some fresh air.

I was in front of the Gare de Lyon. It was already dark and the hands on the giant clock showed five o'clock. I would have liked to jump on a train and arrive very early the next morning in the Midi. It wasn't enough to have left the apartment block without ringing the buzzer on her door. I had to get out of Paris as soon as possible. Unfortunately, I had no more money for a train ticket. I'd given the concierge just about everything in my pouch. What possessed me to pay Death Cheater's debts? But I did remember that in the big apartment near the Bois de Boulogne I was the only one she'd call on when she didn't feel well. After disappearing for several days, she would turn up again with her face all puffy, a crazed look in her eyes. Always at the same time of day, five in the afternoon. And always in the same place, in the living room, on the three steps covered in white plush, which made a sort of dais where she had arranged cushions. She would be lying on the cushions, her face hidden in her hands. And when she heard me coming, she always said the same thing, 'Massage my ankles.' Later, at Fossombronne-la-Forêt, I used to wake up with a start. In my dreams I heard her hoarse voice telling me, 'Massage my ankles.' And, for a few seconds, I thought I was still in the big apartment. It was all going to start happening again.

I didn't feel brave enough to go back down into the metro. I decided to walk home. But I headed off aimlessly, caught up in my own thoughts. I soon realised that I was going round and round the same few connecting streets, all with huge apartment blocks, just beyond the station. Then, at the end of one of those streets, I came out on Boulevard Diderot, from where you can see the passengers coming and going around the station, as well as the illuminated signs: Café Européen.

And Hotel Terminus. I told myself that I should have rented a room in that neighbourhood. Life is completely different when you live near a railway station. It feels as if you're just passing through. Everything is temporary. One day or another, you'll hop on a train. In those neighbourhoods, the future is at your doorstep. All the same, the giant clock face brought back something buried in my past. I think I learned how to tell the time from that clock, back when I was called Little Jewel. I'd already started taking the metro then. It was a direct line from Porte Maillot to Gare de Lyon. I counted the fourteen stations as they passed, so I wouldn't make a mistake. And I would get off at Gare de Lyon, just as I had done earlier today. When I arrived at the top of the steps, I used to check the giant clock face to see that I wasn't late. He would wait for me at the entrance to the metro. Or sometimes at an outside table at the Café Européen. He was my uncle, my mother's brother, or half-brother. At least that's how she introduced him to me. And I often heard her say on the phone, 'My brother will take care of that…I'll send my brother over to you…' Sometimes he looked after me while my mother was away. He would sleep over at the apartment, and take me to school in the morning. Soon I went by myself, then less and less often…On Thursdays and Sundays, I took the metro to the Gare de Lyon to meet him. In the beginning, he would come and pick me up from the apartment in the morning. My mother had told him that he didn't need to go out of his way for me and that I could catch the metro by myself…I don't think he dared defy her wishes, but sometimes, without telling her, he'd wait for me downstairs, outside the apartment block.

It was the first time in ages that I'd walked in that neighbourhood. Was he still living around here? We used to head away from the Gare de Lyon, then turn left into one of the little streets I'd been wandering earlier. At the end of the street, we'd arrive at a tree-lined avenue, where we went into a garage that was always empty. We climbed a staircase to an apartment. We crossed a lobby that opened into a room, in the middle of which was a dining-room table. He didn't have the same last name as my mother, even though they were—apparently—brother and sister.

His name was Jean Borand. There was a photo of him in the biscuit tin and I had recognised him immediately. His name was written in pencil on the back of the photo.

I still felt a constriction in my chest. I would much rather have been thinking about something else. And yet Jean Borand had been kind to me. It wasn't a bad memory, not like the memories of my mother. By now, I had reached Avenue Daumesnil, which reminded me of the street where the garage had been. I walked along, looking from side to side, searching for it. I would ask to speak to 'Monsieur Jean Borand'. From my memory of him, I was certain he would be happy to see me, just like he used to be. Perhaps he wouldn't recognise me? Although he would surely remember me. Was he really my uncle? In any case, he was the only one who would be able to answer my questions. Unfortunately, even though I looked hard at all the buildings on both sides of the street, I didn't recognise anything. There was no garage, not a single landmark. One evening, in the same neighbourhood, near the Gare de Lyon, he had taken me to the cinema. It was my first time. The theatre seemed immense and was showing *The Crossroad of the Archers*, the film in which, a while before, I'd had a small role alongside my mother. I hadn't recognised myself on the screen and, when I'd heard my voice, I'd even wondered if Little Jewel was some other girl, not me.

Yes, I know, it was wrong for me to be thinking about all that, even about Jean Borand. He didn't have anything to do with it, but he, too, was part of that period of my life. That Sunday, I should never have climbed the stairs to the door of the woman who used to be called the Kraut and who is now called Death Cheater. For the moment, I was still walking aimlessly, hoping soon to find Place de la Bastille, where I would take the metro. I tried to cheer myself up: later, after I'd returned to my room, I would go out and telephone Moreau-Badmaev. He'd definitely be home on a Sunday night. I'd suggest that we have dinner together in a café in Place Blanche. I'd tell him everything: about my mother, about Jean Borand, about the apartment near the Bois de Boulogne, and about the girl they used to call Little Jewel. I was still the same person, as if Little Jewel had been preserved, intact, inside a glacier. The same terrifying panic came over me in the street and woke me with a start at five in the morning. And yet I had also experienced long periods of calm, when I ended up forgetting it all. But now that my mother was apparently alive, I no longer knew which path to take.

On a blue street sign I read: AVENUE LEDRU-ROLLIN. It intersected with another street, at the end of which, once again, I caught sight of the massive Gare de Lyon and the illuminated clock face. I'd gone round in circles and come back to where I'd started. The station was a magnet and I was drawn to it; it was a sign of my destiny. I had to get on a train straightaway; I had to *make a break*. The words had suddenly come into my head and I couldn't get rid of them. They gave me a bit more courage. Yes, the time had come to *make a break*. But instead of heading for the station, I kept following Avenue Ledru-Rollin. Before making a break, I had to see this through to the end, without really knowing what *to the end* meant.

There was not another soul around, which was normal for a Sunday night, but the further I walked, the darker the avenue became, as if that evening I had put on sunglasses. Perhaps my eyesight was failing? Further down, on the left-hand side, was the neon sign of a chemist. I didn't take my eyes off it, in case I lost it in the darkness. As long as the green light kept shining, I would be able to find my way. I hoped it would stay lit until I got there. A late-night chemist, that very Sunday, on Avenue Ledru-Rollin. It was so dark that I'd lost all notion of time and thought it was the middle of the night. Behind the shop window, a brunette was sitting at the counter. She wore a white coat and a severe bun, which seemed incompatible with her sweet face. She was sorting a pile of papers and, from time to time, she made notes using a Bic pen with a green lid. Eventually, she would have to notice me staring at her, but I couldn't help myself. Her face was so different from Death Cheater's, the face I had seen in the metro and imagined behind the door on the fourth floor. Anger would never deform the face before me, nor would that mouth ever be contorted or launch a volley of abuse…There was a calmness and grace about her in the soothing glow of the light, the same warm glow I'd experienced in the evenings at Frossombronne-la-Forêt…Had I really experienced that same glow? I pushed open the glass door. I heard the faint tinkling of a bell. She raised her head. I walked towards her, but I didn't know what to say.

'Do you feel ill?'

I couldn't utter a word. And the heaviness in my chest was still suffocating me. She came over to me.

'You're very pale...' She took my hand. I must have given her a fright. And yet her hand felt firm in mine. 'Sit down over here.'

She took me behind the counter, to a room with an old leather armchair. She sat me in the armchair and placed her hand on my forehead.

'You don't have a fever...But your hands are like ice... What's the matter?'

For years I had never said a word to anyone. I had kept it all to myself.

'It would be too complicated to explain,' I replied.

'Why? Nothing is that complicated.'

I burst into tears, which I hadn't done since the dog had died, at least twelve years or so earlier.

'Have you had a shock recently?' she asked, lowering her voice.

'I've seen someone I thought was dead.'

'Someone very close to you?'

'It's not at all important,' I assured her, trying to smile. 'I'm just tired.'

She stood up. I could hear her, back in the shop, opening and shutting a drawer. I was still sitting in the armchair and didn't feel any urge to move.

She came back into the room. She had taken off her white coat to reveal a dark-grey skirt and jumper. She handed me a glass of water, at the bottom of which a red tablet was dissolving in bubbles. She sat next to me, on the arm of the chair.

'Wait until it's properly dissolved.'

I couldn't take my eyes off the fizzing red water. It was phosphorescent.

'What is it?' I asked.

'Something good for you.'

She'd taken my hand in hers again.

'Are your hands still as cold?'

And the way she said 'cold', emphasising the word, suddenly reminded me of the title of a book that Frédérique used to read to me at night, in Frossombronne, when I was in my bed: *The Children of the Cold.*

I downed the drink in one gulp. It tasted bitter. But in my childhood I'd had to swallow pills that were far more bitter.

She went to get a stool from the shop and placed it in front of me so I could rest my legs.

'Try to relax. You don't seem very good at taking it easy.'

She helped me take off my raincoat. Then she unzipped my boots and gently removed them. She came and sat on the arm of the chair again and took my pulse. At the touch of her hand, clasped round my wrist, I immediately felt safe. I could have dropped off to sleep, and that prospect filled me with the same sense of well-being that I experienced when the nuns gave me ether to inhale, and I fell asleep. That was just before I went to live with my mother in the big apartment near the Bois de Boulogne. I was a boarder in a school somewhere and I have no idea why I was waiting in the street that day. No one had come to collect me, so I decided to cross the street, and I was knocked down by a truck. I wasn't badly hurt, only my ankle. They made me lie down in the truck, under the tarpaulin, and drove me to a nearby house. I ended up on a bed, nuns all around, one of them leaning over me. She was wearing a white veil and she gave me inhale ether.

'Do you live in the neighbourhood?'

I told her I lived near Place de Clichy and that I was about to go home on the metro when I'd felt sick. I was on the point of telling her about my visit to the Death Cheater's apartment block in Vincennes but, for her to understand properly, I would have had to go back a long way, perhaps to that afternoon when I was waiting outside the school gate—I'd love to remember exactly where that school was. It wasn't long before everyone had gone home, the pavement was empty, the school gate shut. I was still waiting; no one had come to collect me. Thanks to the ether, I couldn't feel the pain in my ankle anymore, and I drifted off to sleep. A year or two later, in one of the bathrooms in the apartment near the Bois de Boulogne, I came across a bottle of ether. I was mesmerised by the midnight-blue colour of the bottle. Every time my mother had one of her episodes, when she didn't want to see anyone and asked me to bring her meals to her room on a tray or to massage her ankles, I took a whiff from the bottle so I felt brave enough to go to her. It was all too much to explain now. I just wanted to lie there, without speaking, my legs up on the stool.

'Do you feel a bit better?'

I had never met anyone who was so gentle and assured. I had to tell her everything. Did my mother really die in Morocco? The more I went through the biscuit tin, the more doubts crept into my mind. It was the photos that made me uneasy. And especially the one that my mother wanted taken of me in the studio near the Champs-Élysées. She asked the photographer who had just taken a series of shots of her in various poses. I remembered that afternoon well. I was there from the beginning of the session. And the detail in the photos reminded me of the particular accessories that had, I would go so far as to say, *branded* me. The loose-fitting tulle dress that my mother wore belted at the waist; the tight-fitting velvet bodice; and the veil that made her look, under those bright, white camera lights, like a fake fairy. And me, in my dress: I was a fake child prodigy, a poor little circus animal. A toy poodle. Years later, looking at those photos, I finally understood that she was so keen to push me onto the dance floor because then she could make a fresh start herself. She had failed, but it was up to me to become a *star*. Was she really dead? The same old threat was still hanging over my head. But now I had the chance to talk it all through with someone. I didn't even need to say anything. I would show her the photos.

I got up from the armchair. Now was the moment to say something, but I had no idea where to begin.

'Are you sure you're steady on your feet?'

So attentive, her voice so calm. We had left the little room and were back in the shop.

'You should see a doctor. Perhaps you're anaemic.' She looked me in the eye, and smiled. 'The doctor will prescribe vitamin B injections for you. I'm not giving them to you right now…Come back and see me.'

I stood in front of her. I was trying to delay the moment when I'd walk out of the chemist and find myself alone again.

'How are you getting home?'

'On the metro.'

At that time of evening there were plenty of people in the metro. They were on their way home after a movie or a stroll down the Grands Boulevards. I no longer felt up to the metro trip back to my room. This time I was frightened of getting lost for good. And then there was the other problem: if I had to change trains at Châtelet, I did not want to risk coming across that yellow coat again. Everything was going to happen all over again, in the same places, at the same times, until the end. I was trapped in the same old chain of events.

'I'll come with you.'

She saved my life; it was a close call.

She turned off the lights in the chemist and locked the door. The neon sign stayed on. We walked side by side, something I was so unaccustomed to that I could scarcely believe it. I was terrified that, at any moment, I'd wake up in my room. Her hands were in the pockets of her fur coat. I was too scared to take her arm. She was taller than I was.

'What are you thinking about?' she asked.

And she took my arm.

We had reached the intersection that I had crossed

earlier and we were now going down the street at the end of which I could see the Gare de Lyon and the clock.

'I think you're really nice and that I'm wasting your time.'

She turned towards me. The collar of her fur coat brushed her cheek.

'Of course not. You're not wasting my time at all.' She paused for a second. 'I was wondering if your parents are still alive.'

I told her that I still had a mother, who lived in the suburbs.

'And your father?'

My father? He must have been somewhere in the suburbs, too, or in central Paris, or somewhere far away in the big wide world. Or else he died a long time ago.

'I'm not sure about my father's identity.'

I kept my tone casual, as I was worried about making her uneasy. And I wasn't used to confiding in people.

She remained silent. I had shocked her with all that sadness and gloom. I tried to think of something more cheerful, a brighter note.

'But fortunately I was brought up by an uncle who was kind to me.'

It wasn't really a lie. For two or three years, Jean Borand had looked after me every Thursday. Once he had taken me to the Trône fair, not far from his place. Was he my uncle? Perhaps he was my father, after all? When we were living in the apartment near the Bois de Boulogne, my mother used to cover her tracks and embellish the truth. She said to me one day that she 'didn't like vulgar things'; I had no idea what she was referring to. Back when we were living in the big apartment, her name wasn't Suzanne Cardères anymore. She was the Comtesse Sonia O'Dauyé.

'I don't want to bore you with my family stories.'

She still had her arm in mine. We had arrived at the Gare de Lyon, near the metro station. So it was all over now. She would leave me at the top of the stairs.

'I'll take you home in a taxi.'

She led me over to the station. I was so surprised I couldn't bring myself to thank her. There was a line of taxis along the street. Next thing, the taxi driver was waiting for directions. I managed to say, 'Place Blanche.'

The pharmacist asked if I had been living in the neighbourhood for long. No, just a few months. A room in a place on a little street. It used to be a hotel. The rent wasn't much. Besides, I'd found a job. The taxi drove along the river and the empty streets.

'But you've got friends, haven't you?'

At Trois Quartiers, one of my co-workers, Muriel, had introduced me to a small group of people she went out with on Saturday nights. For a little while, I'd been part of the gang. They would go out to dinner and then on to a nightclub. Sales girls, fellows who were starting off at the stock exchange or in jewellery shops or car dealerships. Department managers. One of them seemed more interesting than the others and I went out with him. He used to invite me to dinner and to Studio 28, a cinema in Montmartre, to watch old American movies. One night, after the movie, he took me to a hotel near Châtelet, and I let him have his way. I have only a vague memory of all those people and all those evenings out. None of it mattered at all to me. I couldn't even remember his first name. His surname was all I'd retained: Wurlitzer.

'I don't have many friends anymore,' I said.

'You mustn't be by yourself all the time like that... Otherwise you won't be able to keep fighting your demons.'

She turned and looked at me with a slightly mischievous smile. I couldn't bring myself to ask her how old she was. Perhaps ten or fifteen years older than I was, the same age as my mother at the time of the big apartment and the two photos, of her and of me. All the same, what an odd thing to do, to go and die in Morocco. 'She wasn't a nasty woman,' Frédérique told me one night when we were talking about my mother. 'She was just unlucky.' She had come to Paris when she was very young, to learn classical ballet at the Paris Opera Ballet School. It was all she wanted to do. Then she'd had an accident 'with her ankles' and had to stop ballet. At twenty, she was dancing, but as a chorus girl in obscure cabaret shows, at Ferrari, Préludes, the Moulin Rouge, all those names I'd heard, during their conversations, from the brunette who didn't like my mother and who, like her, had worked in those clubs. 'You see,' Frédérique said, 'because of her ankles, she was like a wounded racehorse on the way to the abattoir.'

The pharmacist leaned over and said, 'Try to cheer up. Shut your eyes and think about pleasant things.' We had reached Rue de Rivoli, before the Louvre, and the taxi was stopped at a red light, even though there were no pedestrians and no other cars. To the right was the illuminated sign of a jazz club, hidden among the dark apartment blocks. Because the bulbs in some of the letters had burned out, you couldn't read the name of the club anymore. I had ended up there one Sunday night, with the others, in a basement where an old orchestra was playing. If we hadn't gone there that night, I guess they would have played to an empty house. Around midnight, I left the club with Wurlitzer, and that was, I believe, the moment when I became aware of just how lonely I was. Rue de Rivoli was empty, a freezing January night...He had suggested that we go to a hotel. I knew the hotel well, with its steep staircase and musty smell. I thought it was the sort of hotel where my mother must have ended up at the same age as me, on the same Sunday nights, when she was called Suzanne Cardères. And I didn't see why everything had to start over again. So I fled. I ran off down Rue de Rivoli under the arcades.

*

I asked the taxi driver to stop on the corner of Boulevard de Clichy. It was time to say goodbye. 'Thank you,' I said to the pharmacist, 'for coming with me.'

I was trying to think of some way I could get her to stay with me. Perhaps it wasn't that late after all. We could have dinner together in the café on Place Blanche.

But she was the one who took the lead. 'I'd really like to see where you live.'

We got out of the taxi and, just as we set off, I felt an odd sensation of lightness. It was the first time I'd walked along that street with someone. Usually, when I came home by myself at night, I would get to the corner of Rue Coustou and suddenly feel like I was leaving the present and sliding into a zone where time had stopped. And I was terrified of never being able to cross back, to return to Place Blanche, where life was being lived. I thought I would remain forever a prisoner of that little street and that room, like Sleeping Beauty. But tonight I had someone with me, and around us was nothing more than a harmless stage set cut out of cardboard. We were walking along the pavement on the right. This time I had taken her arm. She didn't seem at all surprised to be there. We walked the length of the big building at the bottom of the street; we passed the cabaret with the shadowy entrance hall. She looked up at the sign in black letters: ZONE OUT.

'Have you been in there?'

I told her that I hadn't.

'It doesn't look much fun.'

At that time of night, going past Zone Out, I was always

frightened that I'd be dragged into the hallway or, rather, sucked in, as if the laws of gravity no longer applied in that space. Out of superstition, I often walked on the opposite side of the street. The week before, I had dreamed of going to Zone Out. I was sitting there in darkness. A spotlight came on; its cold white light lit up a small stage as well as the room where I found myself at a round table. Sitting at other tables were the silhouettes of motionless men and women who I knew were no longer alive. I woke up with a start. I think I'd been screaming.

We reached number 11 Rue Coustou.

'You'll see…It's quite shabby. And I'm worried that I didn't tidy up.'

'That doesn't matter at all.'

I was being looked after. I no longer felt ashamed or frightened of anything. I went ahead of her on the stairs and along the corridor, but she didn't seem to mind. She followed, nonchalant, as if she knew the way.

I opened the door and switched on the lamp. As luck would have it, I'd made the bed and put my clothes in the wardrobe. There was just my coat hanging from the handle on the window.

She went over to the window. In her soothing voice,

she asked, 'It's not too noisy outside?'

'No, not at all.'

Down below was Rue Puget, a short street that I often took to cut through to Place Blanche. There was a bar on the corner, Le Canter, with yellow wood panelling on the façade. I'd gone there one evening to buy cigarettes. Two dark-haired men were drinking at the bar with a woman. Other men were playing cards in grim silence at a table at the back. I was told that I had to have a drink if I wanted to buy a packet of cigarettes and one of the dark-haired fellows ordered me a whisky, neat, which I downed in one go so I could be done with it. He asked me if I 'lived with my parents'. There really was quite a strange vibe in that place.

She was glued to the window, staring out. I said that it wasn't such a great view. She made a remark about there not being any shutters or curtains. Did I find it difficult to sleep? I assured her that I didn't need curtains. The only thing that would have been really useful was an armchair or even just a chair. But until that evening I had never had any guests.

She sat on the edge of the bed. She wanted to know if I felt better. Yes, I honestly felt much better than earlier, when I had first seen the neon sign of the chemist. Without that landmark, I don't know what would have happened to me.

I wanted to ask her to have dinner with me in the café in Place Blanche. But I didn't have enough money. She was going to leave and I would be alone again in this room. That prospect now seemed even worse than when I was expecting her to let me out of the taxi by myself.

'And how is your job going?'

Perhaps I was deluding myself, but she seemed genuinely concerned about me.

'I work with a friend,' I said. 'We translate broadcasts made by foreign radio stations.'

What would Moreau-Badmaev have made of that lie? But I didn't want to tell her about the Taylor Agency, about Véra Valadier, or her husband, or the little girl. It all seemed too frightening to think about.

'Do you know many foreign languages?'

And I could see in her eyes that I had gained a measure of respect. I wished it weren't a lie.

'It's my friend who knows most of them…I'm still a student at the School of Oriental Languages.'

Student. The word had always impressed me, while actually being one seemed somehow out of my reach. I don't think the Kraut had even graduated from primary school. She made spelling mistakes, but they weren't so obvious because she had such big handwriting. As for me, I'd left school at fourteen.

'So, you're a student?'

She seemed relieved for me. I wanted to put her mind at rest even more, so I added, 'It was my uncle who advised me to enrol at the School of Oriental Languages. He's a teacher himself.'

And I conjured up an apartment in the university neighbourhood, which I barely knew and which, in my mind, was somewhere in the vicinity of the Pantheon. And there was my uncle, at his desk, by the light of a reading lamp, hunched over an old book.

'What does he teach?' She smiled at me. Had she really been taken in by my lie?

'Philosophy.'

I thought of the man I used to meet every Thursday, when we were living in the big apartment, my uncle—that's what we called him—the so-called Jean Borand. We used to enjoy listening to the echo of our voices in the old empty garage. He was young and had a Parisian accent. He'd taken me to see *The Crossroad of the Archers.* He'd also taken me to the Trône fair, not far from the garage. He always wore a tie pin and, on his right wrist, a chain bracelet, which he said was a present from my mother. He called her Suzanne. He would never have understood why I claimed he was a philosophy teacher. Why lie? Especially to this woman who appeared to be so favourably disposed to me.

'I'm going to let you sleep now…'

'Couldn't you stay the night with me?'

It was as if someone else was speaking. I was terribly surprised at having been so bold. I was ashamed.

She didn't bat an eyelid. 'Are you frightened of being here alone?'

She was still sitting on the edge of the bed, next to me, looking me in the eye, and her gaze, unlike my mother's in the painting by Tola Soungouroff, was gentle.

'I'll stay if that would be a comfort to you.'

And, with weary, unaffected ease, she took off her shoes. It was as if she did the same thing every evening, at the same time, in this same room. She lay back, without taking off her fur coat. I remained on the edge of the bed, motionless.

'You should lie down, too. You need some sleep.'

I lay down next to her. I didn't know what to say or, rather, I was frightened that the slightest word would sound false, and that she'd change her mind, get up and leave. She was silent, too. I heard music nearby; it sounded as if it was coming from in front of the building. Someone was playing a percussion instrument. The notes rang out, clear and mournful, like background music.

'Do you think it's coming from Zone Out?' she said. And she burst out laughing. Suddenly, it all dropped away: everything that terrified me, made me uneasy and led me to believe that, ever since I was a child, I could never shake off an evil curse. A musician with a thin lacquered moustache was tapping a xylophone with his drumsticks. And I envisioned the stage at Zone Out, illuminated by the cold white spotlight. A man dressed as a coach driver was cracking his whip and announcing in a muffled voice, 'And now, ladies and gentlemen, I give you Death Cheater!'

The lights faded. And suddenly, under the spotlight, the woman in the yellow coat appeared, just as I had seen her in the metro. She walked slowly towards the front of the stage. The fellow with the lacquered moustache kept banging his instrument with his drumsticks. She greeted the audience with her arms raised. But there was no audience. Just a few inert, mummified figures seated at some round tables.

'Yes,' I said. 'The music must be coming from Zone Out.'

She asked if she could turn off the light on the bedside table, which was on her side of the bed.

The neon light from the garage shone its familiar glow on the wall above us. I started to cough. She moved over, closer to me. I rested my head on her shoulder. As soon as I felt the fur's softness, my anxiety and dark thoughts began to recede. Little Jewel, Death Cheater, the Kraut, the yellow coat...All those pathetic props now belonged to someone else's life. I had shed them like a costume, a harness I had been made to wear for ages and which made it difficult to breathe. I felt her lips on my forehead.

'I don't like you coughing like that,' she said softly. 'You must have caught a cold in this room.'

She was right. It would soon be winter and they hadn't yet turned on the central heating.

SHE LEFT VERY early the next morning. I had to go to Neuilly that afternoon to look after the little girl. I rang the doorbell of the Valadier home at around three o'clock. Véra Valadier opened the door and seemed surprised to see me. It was as if I'd woken her up and she'd had to get dressed quickly.

'I didn't know you came on Thursdays as well.'

And when I asked if the little girl was there, Véra Valadier said no. Her daughter wasn't home from school yet. Even though it was Thursday and there was no school. But she explained that on Thursday afternoons the boarders played in the playground and the little girl was with them. I had noticed that neither Véra Valadier nor her husband ever called her by her name. They both referred to her as 'she'.

And when they called out for their daughter, they merely said, 'Where are you? What are you doing?' They never uttered her first name. After all these years, I couldn't tell you now what that name was. I've forgotten it, and I wonder if I ever even knew it.

She took me into the ground-floor room where Monsieur Valadier usually made his phone calls, sitting on the corner of his desk. Why, I couldn't help asking, on her daughter's day off school, had she left her there with the boarders?

'But she really enjoys staying back there on Thursday afternoons…'

In the past, my mother used to say things like that, and always when I was so distraught that all I wanted to do was inhale the bottle of ether.

'You can go and collect her later…Otherwise she'll be perfectly happy to come home by herself. Will you excuse me for a moment?'

Judging by her voice and her expression, she seemed to be somewhat upset. She disappeared in a hurry, leaving me in that room without a single chair. I was tempted to sit, like Monsieur Valadier, on the corner of the desk. It was gigantic, leather-topped, made out of light-coloured wood, with two drawers on either side, and not a single sheet of paper or even a pencil on top. Only a telephone. Perhaps Monsieur Valadier kept his files in the drawers. My curiosity got the better of me and I opened and shut the drawers in turn. They were empty, except that at the back of one I found a few business cards with the name Michel Valadier, but the address was not in Neuilly.

Sounds of an argument were coming from upstairs. I recognised Madame Valadier's voice, and I was surprised to hear her shouting and swearing, but, every now and again, her voice became plaintive. There was the sound of a man's voice answering her. They passed in front of the doorway. Madame Valadier's voice became softer. Now they were speaking very quietly in the lobby. Then the front door banged shut and, from the window, I watched as a dark-haired, quite short young man wearing a suede jacket and a scarf headed off.

Madame Valadier came back into the study. 'My apologies for deserting you…' She approached me and I could tell by her expression that she wanted to ask me something. 'Would you be able to help me do some tidying up?'

She led me to the stairs and I went up to the first floor behind her. We entered a big bedroom, at the end of which was a wide, low bed. It was the only item of furniture in the room. The bed was unmade, and there was a tray resting beside it, with two champagne glasses and an open bottle of champagne. A cork lay conspicuously in the middle of the grey carpet. The bedspread was hanging off the end of the bed. The sheets were tangled, the pillows scattered all over the bed, where a man's dressing-gown in dark-blue silk had been tossed, along with a camisole and knickers and a pair of stockings. An ashtray filled with butts was on the floor.

Madame Valadier went to open the two windows. There was a sickly smell hanging in the air, a mixture of perfume and Virginia tobacco, the smell of people who have spent a long time in the same room and the same bed.

She picked up the blue dressing-gown. 'I have to put this back in my husband's wardrobe,' she said.

When she came back, she asked if I wanted to help her make the bed. She pulled up the sheets and blanket. Her movements were abrupt and rapid, as if she was frightened of being caught out by someone, and I had trouble keeping up with her. She hid the lingerie and stockings under a pillow. As we finished straightening the bedspread, she caught sight of the tray.

'Oh, yes, I'd forgotten about that...'

She picked up the bottle of champagne and the two glasses and opened a wardrobe where lots of pairs of shoes were lined up on shelves. I had never seen so many shoes: different-coloured court shoes, ballerina flats, boots...She shoved the bottle and glasses at the back of the top shelf and shut the wardrobe. She looked like someone rushing to hide compromising evidence before the police arrived. All that was left now were the ashtray and the champagne cork. I picked them up. She took them out of my hands and went into the bathroom. The door was open and I heard the noise of the toilet flushing.

She looked at me strangely. She wanted to say something, but she didn't have time. Through the open windows, we could hear a diesel engine. She leaned out one of the windows. I was right behind her. Down below, Monsieur Valadier was getting out of a taxi. He was carrying an overnight bag and a black leather briefcase.

When we went down to join him, he was already on the phone, sitting on his desk, and he greeted us with a wave. Then he hung up. Madame Valadier asked him if his trip had gone well.

'Not great, Véra.'

She shook her head, absorbed. 'But you're not worried, are you?'

'Overall, things are fine, but there are still a few sticking points.'

He turned to me and smiled. 'Isn't she at school today?'

He was referring to his daughter, but I got the impression that he wasn't really interested and that he was merely asking out of politeness to me.

'I let her stay at school with the boarders,' said Madame Valadier.

Monsieur Valadier took off his navy-blue coat and placed it on his overnight bag, on the floor by the desk.

'You know, she can just as easily come home by herself…' He spoke softly, still smiling at me. He had the same attitude as his wife.

'There's something we want to discuss with you about our daughter,' said Madame Valadier. 'She'd like to have a dog.'

Monsieur Valadier was still sitting on the corner of his desk. He was swinging one leg in a steady rhythm. Where on earth could people sit if they came to meet him in this office? I wondered. Although I was pretty sure that no one ever came here.

'You'll have to explain to her that it's not possible,' Véra Valadier said. She seemed aghast at the idea that a dog might turn up in the house. 'Will you tell her later?'

She looked so anxious that I couldn't help myself from saying, 'Yes, madame.'

She smiled at me. That had clearly taken a load off her mind.

'I've already asked you to call me Véra, not madame.'

She was standing next to her husband, leaning against the desk.

'In fact, it would be much simpler if you just called us Véra and Michel.'

Her husband was smiling at me, too. There they were, across the room, with their smooth, unlined faces, still quite young.

For me, the evil curse and the bad memories all centred on one face, that of my mother. The little girl had to contend with these two individuals whose smiles and smooth skin were of the kind we're sometimes shocked to see on the faces of murderers who have long remained unpunished.

Monsieur Valadier removed a cigarillo from the top pocket of his jacket and lit it with his lighter. He took a puff and exhaled thoughtfully.

'I'm counting on you to sort out this dog business.'

*

I saw the little girl at once. She was sitting on the bench, reading a magazine. Around her, twenty or so older girls were scattered about the schoolyard. The boarders. She wasn't paying them the slightest attention, as if she had been waiting there all day without any idea why. She seemed surprised that I had come to collect her so early.

We went down Rue de la Ferme.

'We don't have to go home straightaway,' she said.

We had reached the end of the street and we set off into the section of the Bois de Boulogne where there are pine trees. It was odd to be walking on a late-November afternoon among trees that were reminiscent of summer and the sea. When I was her age, I didn't want to go home either. And could you even call it a home, that gigantic apartment where I had ended up with my mother, without it ever being clear to me why she was living there? The first time she took me there, I thought it belonged to some friends of hers, and I was surprised when the two of us stayed the night—'I'm going to show you your room,' she announced. And I was anxious when I had to go to bed. In that big empty room with the oversized bed, I expected someone to come and ask me what I was doing there. It was as if I had intuited that my mother and I were not really supposed to be on the premises.

'Have you been living in that house for long?' I asked the little girl.

She had been there at the beginning of the year. But she couldn't remember exactly where she was living before that. What had struck me, the first time I went to the Valadier house, were all those empty rooms, which reminded me of the apartment where I'd lived with my mother when I was the same age as the little girl. I recalled that, in the kitchen, there was a board stuck on the wall, with white panels that lit up, the words in black lettering: DINING ROOM, STUDY and so on. I also recalled the words CHILDREN'S BEDROOM. Who could those children possibly be? They were probably going to come back at any moment and ask me why I was in their bedroom.

It was dusk and the little girl was still keen to delay our return. We had headed off in the other direction from her parents' home. But was it really their home? Twelve years on, who still knew, for example, that my mother had also lived in Avenue Malakoff, very near the Bois de Boulogne? That apartment didn't belong to us. I found out later that my mother was staying there while the owner was away. Frédérique and one of her women friends talked about it one evening at Fossombronne-la-Fôret, over dinner, when I was at the table. Certain words stick in children's minds and, even if they don't understand them at the time, they understand them twenty years later. It's a bit like the grenades we were told to watch out for at Fossombronne-la-Fôret. Apparently, ever since the war, there were one or two buried in Kraut's Field, and there was still a chance they could explode after all this time.

Yet another reason to be frightened. But we couldn't resist slipping out to that overgrown vacant block and playing hide-and-seek. Frédérique had gone to the apartment to try to find something my mother had forgotten when she left.

We had arrived at the edge of the little lake where people came to ice-skate in winter. The twilight was beautiful. The trees were outlined against a blue and pink sky.

'So, you'd like a dog.'

She was embarrassed, as if I had revealed her secret.

'Your parents told me.'

She frowned and pursed her lips, pouting. 'They don't want a dog,' she said.

'I'm going to try to speak to them about it. They'll come round sooner or later.'

She smiled at me. She seemed to trust me. She believed that I'd be able to persuade Véra and Michel Valadier. But I was under no illusion about those two: they were as tough as the Kraut. I had suspected as much from the beginning. With Véra, it was immediately obvious. She had a fake first name. And, in my opinion, his name wasn't Michel Valadier, either. He must have already gone by several other names. And, indeed, there was a different address on his business card. I wondered if he wasn't even more devious and more dangerous than his wife.

Now we had to head home, and I was regretting my empty promise to her. We were walking along the riding tracks to get back to the Jardin d'Acclimatation. I was certain that Véra and Michel Valadier wouldn't give in.

He opened the front door and went straight back to his study on the ground floor, without saying a word to us. I heard gales of raucous, vicious laughter. Madame Valadier—Véra—was yelling, but I couldn't make out what she was saying. Their voices were indistinguishable, each trying to shout over the top of the other. The little girl opened her eyes wide. She was frightened, but I sensed that she was used to this fear. In the lobby, she stood still, frozen; I should have taken her off somewhere else. But where? Madame Valadier came out of the study, looking calm and composed.

'Did you have a nice walk?' she asked.

Once again, she looked like those cold, mysterious blondes who glide through old American movies. Then Monsieur Valadier came out. He was also very calm. He was wearing an elegant black suit and there were big scratches down one of his cheeks, most likely from fingernails. Véra Valadier's fingernails? She kept hers rather long. The two of them were standing next to each other in the doorway, with their smooth faces of murderers who would remain unpunished, for lack of evidence. It looked as if they were posing for a photo, not for an official identity shot but for the cameras at the beginning of a soirée, as the guests arrive.

'Did mademoiselle explain about the dog?' asked Véra Valadier. Her tone was distant, not at all like the voices you hear around Rue de Douai, where she'd told me she was born. With another first name.

'Dogs are sweet,' she said. 'But they're very dirty.'

'Your maman is right,' Michel Valadier added, in the same tone as his wife. 'It would really not be a good idea to have a dog in the house.'

'When you're a big girl, you'll be able to have all the dogs you like…But not here and not now.'

Véra Valadier's voice had changed. She sounded bitter. Perhaps she was imagining a time in the future—time passes so quickly—when her daughter would be grown up and when she, Véra, would roam the corridors of the metro forever and ever, in a yellow coat.

The little girl didn't say a thing. She merely stared, wide-eyed.

'You see, with dogs you get diseases,' Monsieur Valadier said. 'And, well, they bite, too.'

Now he had a shifty look and an odd way of speaking, like an illegal street peddler keeping an eye out for the police.

I was finding it hard to remain quiet. I would gladly have stood up for the little girl, but I didn't want the conversation to get poisonous and for her then to get scared. Nevertheless, I couldn't stop myself from looking Michel Valadier straight in the eye. 'Did you hurt yourself, sir?'

I touched my finger to my cheek, the same spot where

the long scratches ran down his cheek.

'No...Why?' he muttered.

'You really should put some disinfectant on that. It's like a dog bite. You can catch rabies.'

This time, I could tell he was out of his depth. And Véra Valadier was, too. They were looking at me warily. Under the glare of the chandelier, thrown off course, they were nothing but a suspicious couple who had just been rounded up in a raid.

'I think we're late,' she said, turning to her husband.

She had recovered her cold voice. Michel Valadier checked his bracelet watch.

'Yes, we must go,' he agreed, also feigning indifference.

'There's a slice of ham for you in the fridge,' she said to the little girl. 'I think we'll be home late tonight...'

The little girl drew nearer to me and took my hand, squeezing it like someone who wanted to be guided through the darkness.

'It would be better if you left,' Madame Valadier said. 'She has to get used to being by herself.' She took the little girl by the hand and pulled her away. 'Mademoiselle is going to leave now. You're to have dinner and put yourself to bed.'

The little girl looked at me once more, her eyes wide,

as if she would never again be astonished by anything. Michel Valadier had moved in closer, and the little girl was now standing motionless between her parents.

'See you tomorrow,' I said to her.

'See you tomorrow.'

But she didn't seem very sure about it.

*

Outside, I sat down on a bench beside the path that runs along the Jardin d'Acclimatation. I had no idea what I was waiting for. After a while, I saw Madame and Monsieur Valadier leave the house. She was wearing a fur coat; he had on his navy-blue coat. They didn't walk close together. When they reached the black car, she got in the back seat and he took the wheel, as if he were her chauffeur. The car headed off towards Avenue de Madrid, and I realised that I would never know anything about these people, neither their real first names nor their real surnames, nor why a troubled look sometimes came over Madame Valadier, nor why there were no chairs in Monsieur Valadier's study, nor why the address on his business card was different from that of his office at home. And the little girl? She, at least, was not a mystery to me. I intuited what she might have been feeling. I had been, more or less, the same sort of child.

A light came on in her room on the second floor. I was tempted to go and keep her company. I thought I saw her shadow at the window. But I didn't ring the doorbell. I was feeling so miserable around that time that I scarcely felt up to helping someone else. What's more, the business with the dog had reminded me of an incident in my own childhood.

I walked to the Porte Maillot, relieved to get out of the Bois de Boulogne. During the day, when I was with the little girl at the edge of the skaters' lake, I could just about bear it. But, now that it was night, I felt a sensation of emptiness which was far more horrific than the vertigo that overwhelmed me on the pavement in Rue Coustou, outside Zone Out.

On my right, the first trees marked the entrance to the Bois de Boulogne. One November evening, a dog went missing in that park; it was something I would be haunted by for the rest of my life, at times when I least expected it. During sleepless nights and lonely days, and even during summer. I should have explained to the little girl how dangerous it was, this business of having a dog.

When I entered the schoolyard earlier and saw her

sitting on the bench, I thought back to another schoolyard. I was the same age as the little girl and there were older boarders in that schoolyard, too. They took care of us. Every morning, they helped us to get dressed and, in the evening, to get ready for bed. They mended our clothes. My 'big girl' was called Thérèse, like me. She had dark hair and blue eyes, and a tattoo on her arm. As I recall, she looked a bit like the pharmacist. The other boarders, and even the nuns, were wary of her, but she was always kind to me. She stole chocolate from the kitchen and sneaked it to me at night in the dormitory. During the day, she sometimes took me to a studio, not far from the chapel, where the big girls were learning how to iron.

One day, my mother came to collect me. She told me to get in the car and I sat on the front bench seat, next to her. I think she told me that I was never going back to that boarding school. There was a dog on the back seat. And the car was parked almost at the same spot where I'd been knocked down by the truck, not long before. The boarding school can't have been far from the Gare de Lyon. I remember, when Jean Borand used to wait for me outside the boarding school on Sundays, we would walk to his garage. And the day my mother took me away in the car with the dog, we went past the Gare de Lyon. In those days, the streets were deserted and I had the impression that the two of us in the car were the only people in Paris.

That was the day I went with her, for the first time, to the huge apartment near the Bois de Boulogne, the day she showed me MY ROOM. Before then, the few times Jean Borand took me to see her, we went by metro to the Place de l'Étoile, where she was still living in a hotel. Her room was smaller than my room in Rue Coustou. In the metal box, I found a telegram addressed to her at that hotel and in her real name: Suzanne Cardères, Hôtel San Remo, 8 Rue d'Armaillé. I was relieved every time I discovered the actual address of those places I only vaguely remembered, but which appeared in my nightmares over and over again. If I knew their exact location and studied their façades, I was convinced they would become less threatening.

A dog. A black poodle. Right from the start, he slept in my room. My mother never looked after him and, moreover, would have been no more capable of looking after a dog than a child. No doubt someone had given her the dog as a present. For her, it was nothing more than a fashion accessory that she must have got bored with quickly. I still wonder by what twist of fate that dog and I ended up together in the car. Now that she was living in the huge apartment and her name was Sonia O'Dauyé, she probably needed a dog and a little girl.

I used to go for walks with the dog, beyond the apartment block and all the way along the avenue, down to the Porte Maillot. I can't recall the dog's name. It wasn't a name my mother had given him. It was around the beginning of the time I went to live with her in the apartment. She hadn't yet enrolled me in the Saint-André school and I wasn't yet known as Little Jewel. Jean Borand collected me on Thursdays and took me to his garage for the whole day. And I kept the dog with me. I knew already that my mother would forget to feed him. I was the one who got food ready for him. When Jean Borand came to collect me, we took the metro, and smuggled the dog onto the train, too. We walked from the Gare de Lyon to the garage. I wanted to remove his leash. There was no chance of him getting run over; there were no cars in the streets. But Jean Borand warned me not to take off his leash. After all, I had almost got run over by a truck in front of the school.

My mother enrolled me in Saint-André. I walked there alone every morning, and I came home every evening at around six. Unfortunately, I couldn't take the dog to school, even though it was very close to the apartment, on Rue Pergolèse. I found the exact address on a scrap of paper in my mother's diary. Cours Saint-André, 58 Rue Pergolèse. On whose advice did she send me to that place? I stayed there all day long.

One evening, when I got home to the apartment, the dog wasn't there. I thought my mother had gone out with him. She had promised me that she'd walk him and feed him, tasks I'd already asked the cook to do, the Chinese man who prepared dinner and brought my mother a breakfast tray to her room every morning. My mother came home a bit later, without the dog. She said she'd lost it in the Bois de Boulogne. She had the leash in her bag and she handed it to me as if to prove that she wasn't lying. Her voice was very calm. She didn't look sad. She seemed to think it was all quite normal. 'You'll have to make up a lost-dog notice tomorrow, and perhaps someone will return him.' She took me to my room. But her tone was so calm, so blasé, that I had the feeling she was preoccupied with something else. I was the only one who thought about the dog. No one ever brought him back. I was too scared to turn out the light in my room. Since the dog had been sleeping with me, I wasn't used to being by myself at night, and now it was even worse than at boarding school. I pictured him in the darkness, lost in the middle of the Bois de Boulogne. That same evening, my mother went out, and I still remember the dress she was wearing. It was a blue dress with a veil. That dress has appeared in my nightmares for a long time, always worn by a skeleton.

I kept the light on all that night, and every other night. I never stopped being frightened. It would be my turn after the dog's, I was sure of it.

Strange thoughts came into my mind, so muddled that I waited ten or so years for them to take shape, before I could put them into words. One morning, sometime before seeing the woman in the yellow coat in the corridors of the metro, I woke up with a sentence running through my head, one of those sentences which seem incomprehensible, because they are the last shreds of a forgotten dream: *You had to kill the Kraut to avenge the dog.*

I GOT HOME to my room in Rue Coustou around seven in the evening, and I wasn't up to waiting until Wednesday for the pharmacist to come back. She was out of town for a couple of days. She had given me a telephone number in case I needed to speak to her: 225 Bar-sur-Aube.

In the basement of the café in Place Blanche, I asked the cloakroom woman to dial 225 Bar-sur-Aube for me. But the second she picked up the receiver, I told her not to bother. All of a sudden, I could no longer bring myself to disturb the pharmacist. I bought a token, went into the booth, and ended up calling Moreau-Badmaev's number. He was listening to a program on the radio, but he asked me to come over anyway. I was relieved to know that someone was happy to spend the evening with me. I was loath to take the metro to the Porte d'Orléans. I was scared of changing trains at Montparnasse-Bienvenue. The corridor was as long as the one at Châtelet, and there wasn't a moving walkway. I had enough money to take a taxi there. Once I was in the taxi at the top of the line in front of the Moulin Rouge, I suddenly felt at ease, just as I had the other evening with the pharmacist.

*

The green light of the radio set was switched on, and Moreau-Badmaev was sitting against the wall, writing on a pad, while a man with a tinny voice spoke in a foreign language. This time, he said, he didn't need to write in shorthand. The man was speaking so slowly that he had time to write out the words. Tonight, he was doing it for pleasure and not at all for work-related reasons. It was a poetry reading. The program was being transmitted from somewhere faraway, and from time to time the man's voice was muffled by static. He stopped talking and some harp music came on. Badmaev held out a piece of paper that I have treasured to this day:

Mar egy hete csak a mamara
Gondolok mindig, meg-megallva.

Nyikorgo kosarral öleben,
Ment a padlasra, ment serénye n

En meg öszinte ember voltam,
Orditottam toporzékoltam.
Hagyja a dagadt ruhat masra
Emgem vigyen föl a padlasra

He translated the poem for me, but I've forgotten what it meant and what language it was written in. Then he lowered the volume on the radio, but the green light stayed on.

'You seem a little out of sorts.'

He was looking at me so considerately that I felt at ease, just as I had with the pharmacist. I wanted to tell him everything. I described the afternoon I'd spent with the little girl in the Bois de Boulogne, Véra and Michel Valadier, going back to my room in the Rue Coustou. And the dog that was lost forever almost twelve years ago. He asked me what colour the dog was.

'Black.'

'And have you spoken to your mother about it since?'

'I haven't seen her since then. I thought she'd died in Morocco.'

I was ready to tell him about coming across the woman with the yellow coat in the metro, about the large apartment block in Vincennes, the staircase and Death Cheater's door, where I hadn't been bold enough to knock.

'I had an odd childhood...'

He listened to the radio all day long, taking notes on his writing pad. So he might as well listen to me.

'When I was seven years old, they called me Little Jewel.'

He smiled at me. He probably thought that was a delightful name for a little girl. I bet his mother gave him a nickname that she whispered in his ear before kissing him goodnight. Patoche. Pinky. Poulou.

'It's not what you think,' I said. 'It was my stage name.'

He frowned. He didn't understand. At that time, my mother also had a stage name: Sonia O'Dauyé. After a while, she had given up using her assumed title, but the little copper plaque, which read COMTESSE SONIA O'DAUYÉ, had remained on the apartment door.

'Your stage name?'

I wondered if I should start from the beginning and tell him everything. My mother's arrival in Paris, the ballet school, the hotel on Rue Coustou, then the one on

Rue d'Armaillé, and my own first memories: the boarding school, the truck and the ether, that period when I wasn't yet called Little Jewel. But I had revealed my stage name to him, so it was better that I stick to when my mother and I ended up in the big apartment. It wasn't enough for her to have lost a dog in the Bois de Boulogne. She had to have something else that she could show off like a piece of jewellery: that's no doubt why she gave me my name.

He remained silent. Perhaps he thought that I was now diffident about continuing, or that I had lost track of my story. I didn't dare look at him. I stared at the green light in the middle of the radio set, a soothing phosphorescent green.

'I'll have to show you some photos...Then you'll understand better.'

And I tried to describe the two photos taken on the same day, the two head shots: 'Sonia O'Dauyé and Little Jewel', taken for a film in which my mother had been hired to perform, having never been a professional actress before. Why was she hired? And by whom? She wanted me to play the role of her daughter in this film. She was not the leading actress, but she insisted that I stay close to her. I had replaced the dog. For how long?

'What was the name of this film?'

'The Crossroad of the Archers.'

I replied without hesitation, but they were like words we learn off by heart in childhood—a prayer or a song recited from beginning to end without our ever really grasping the meaning.

'Do you remember the shoot?'

I had to arrive very early in the morning. It was a sort of huge warehouse. Jean Borand had taken me there. Later, in the afternoon, when I had finished and could leave, he had driven me to the nearby Buttes-Chaumont park. It was very hot: it was summer. I had performed my part; I never had to go back to the warehouse again.

I had to lie on a bed, then sit up and say, 'I'm scared.' It was as simple as that. Another day, I had to keep lying on the bed and flip through a photo album. Then my mother came into the bedroom, wearing a diaphanous blue dress—the same dress she was wearing when she left the apartment on the evening after losing the dog. She sat on the bed and looked at me with big sad eyes. Then she caressed my cheek and leaned over to kiss me; I remember we had to do it several times. In everyday life, she never showed the slightest bit of affection.

He was listening closely, and wrote something on his pad. I asked him what it was.

'The title of the film. It would be fun for you to see it again, don't you think?'

Over the past twelve years, the idea of seeing the film again had not even occurred to me. For me, it was as if it had never existed. I had never mentioned it to anyone.

'Do you think it would be possible to see it?'

'I've got a friend who works at the cinematheque. I'll ask him.'

Now I was worried. I was like a criminal who, with time, forgets her crime, even though incriminating evidence remains. She lives under another identity and her appearance is so changed that no one recognises her. If someone had asked me, 'You weren't Little Jewel, were you, a while ago?' I would have replied no, and I would not have felt as if I were lying. That July day when my mother took me to the Gare d'Austerlitz and hung the label around my neck—Thérèse Cardères, c/o Mme Chatillon, Chemin du Bréau, Fossombronne-la Forêt—I knew it would be best to forget Little Jewel. Indeed, my mother had made a point of telling me not to speak to anyone or say where I had lived in Paris. I was simply a boarder coming back on holiday to her family in Chemin du Bréau, Fossombronne-la-Forêt. The train left. It was crowded and I was standing up in the aisle. It was lucky I was wearing my label, otherwise I would have got lost among all those people. I would have forgotten my name.

'I don't really want to see the film,' I said.

The other morning, I'd been terrified by something I heard a woman say at the next table, in the café at Place Blanche: 'The skeleton in the cupboard.' I felt like asking Moreau-Badmaev if, over time, film stock decomposes like corpses. In that case, the faces of Sonia O'Dauyé and Little Jewel would be eaten away by some sort of fungus and their voices would not be heard again.

*

He told me I looked pale and suggested that we have dinner nearby.

We walked down the left-hand side of Boulevard Jourdan and entered a large café. He chose a table in the indoor terrace.

'Look, we're right opposite the Cité Universitaire.' He pointed to a building on the other side of the boulevard that looked like a castle. 'The students from Cité Universitaire come here and, because they speak all sorts of languages, they call this café Babel.'

I looked around the café. It was late and there weren't many people.

'I often come here and listen to people speaking their different languages. It's good practice for me. There are even Iranian students but, unfortunately, none of them speaks Persian of the plains.'

At that time of night, they were no longer serving meals, so he ordered two sandwiches.

'And what would you like to drink?'

'A whisky, neat.'

It was at about this time the other night when I'd gone to Le Canter, in Rue Puget, to buy cigarettes. And I remembered how much better I'd felt after they'd made me drink the glass of whisky. I could breathe better; the anxiety had dissipated, along with the heaviness that was suffocating me. It was almost as good as the ether from my childhood.

'You must have had a good education.'

I was worried that my voice might be tinged with envy or bitterness.

'Only the baccalaureate and the School of Oriental Languages.'

'Do you think I could enrol in the School of Oriental Languages?'

'Of course.'

So I would not have told a complete lie to the pharmacist.

'Did you pass the bac?'

At first I wanted to say yes, but it was too stupid to lie again now that I had confided in him.

'No, unfortunately.'

I must have looked so ashamed and upset that he shrugged his shoulders. 'It doesn't really matter, you know. Lots of amazing people don't have their bac.'

I tried to remember all the schools I'd been to: the boarding school, to begin with, from the age of five, where the big kids looked after us. What had happened to Thérèse since that time, long ago? She had at least one distinguishing feature I would have recognised: the tattoo on her shoulder, which she told me was a starfish. And then I'd been to Saint-André, when I lived with my mother in the big apartment. But, after a while, she started calling me Little Jewel and wanted me to have a role alongside her in the film, *The Crossroad of the Archers*. I was no longer attending Saint-André. I also remember a young man who looked after me for a very short time. Perhaps my mother had found him through the red-headed fellow at the Taylor Agency who had sent me to the Valadiers. One winter, when it was snowing heavily in Paris, the young man took me tobogganing in the Trocadéro gardens.

'Aren't you hungry?'

I had just drunk a mouthful of whisky and he was looking at me anxiously. I hadn't touched my sandwich.

'You should eat something.'

I forced myself to take a bite, but I had real trouble swallowing. I drank another mouthful of whisky. I wasn't used to alcohol. It tasted bitter, but it had started to take effect.

'Do you often drink spirits?'

'No. Not often. Only tonight, so I could pluck up the courage to talk.'

I would show him the photo from *The Crossroad of the Archers* that I had filed away at the bottom of the metal tin. I avoided looking at it. I was wearing a nightshirt, wide-eyed, an electric torch in my hand, and I was wandering around the corridors of the château. I'd left my room because of the storm.

'There's one thing I don't understand. Why did your

mother leave you and go to Morocco?'

It was odd to hear someone asking these questions, when up until now I had been the only one to ask them of myself. Sometimes, in the Fossombronne house, I had overheard snatches of conversation between Frédérique and her friends. They thought I was out of earshot or that I was too young to understand. Some words have remained etched in my memory—especially those of the brunette, the one who had known my mother from the early days and who didn't like her. One day I heard her say, 'It's lucky Sonia left Paris in time...' I must have been thirteen and I was puzzled, but I didn't dare ask Frédérique to explain.

'I don't really know,' I said. 'I think she went there with someone.'

Yes, she'd been taken there by a man, or he'd asked her to join him there. Was it Jean Borand? I don't think so. He would have suggested that I go along, too. One evening, while Frédérique was out, the women were talking about my mother again, and the brunette said, 'Sonia went out with some very weird types.' One of them had paid—so she said—'for Sonia to be in a movie'. I realised it was *The Crossroad of the Archers*.

One afternoon in summer, I'd gone for a walk in the

forest with Frédérique. We went down Chemin du Bréau, which led to the forest. I asked her why, out of the blue, my mother had ended up in the huge apartment. Apparently, she had met someone and he had set her up there. But nobody ever knew what his name was. He was probably the one who took her to Morocco. Later on, I imagined a faceless man carrying suitcases at night. Secret meetings in hotel lobbies, on railway platforms, and always under the bluish tinge of a streetlight. Trucks being loaded in empty garages, like Jean Borand's, near the Gare de Lyon. And the smell of rotting leaves and decomposition, the smell of the Bois de Boulogne on the evening when she lost the dog.

*

It must have been late, because the waiter came over to tell us that it was closing time.

'Do you want to come back to my place?' Moreau-Badmaev asked.

Perhaps he'd sensed what was on my mind. At the prospect of finding myself alone that night in Porte d'Orléans, I'd again felt something pressing down on me, preventing me from breathing.

Back at his apartment, he offered me a hot drink. I heard him opening and shutting a cupboard, boiling water; then there was the sound of a saucepan banging. If I lay on the mattress for a second, I would feel better. A warm, hazy light emanated from the globe in the tripod. I would have liked to turn on the radio set to see the green light. Now that I was lying down, my head on the pillow—a much softer pillow than I was used to at Rue Coustou—I felt as if someone had removed a metal or plaster corset from my chest. I wanted to spend all day like that, far from Paris, in the Midi, or in Rome, with sunlight filtering through the slats of the louvres.

He came into the room holding a tray. I sat up. I was embarrassed.

'No, no, stay where you are,' he said, and put the tray on the ground, at the foot of the mattress.

He handed me a cup. Then he pushed the pillow behind me and wedged it against the wall so I could lean back on it.

'You should take off your coat.'

I wasn't even aware that I still had my coat on. And my shoes. I put the cup down on the floor next to me. He helped me take off my coat and shoes. When he took off my shoes, I felt a huge relief, as if he'd removed the sort of leg irons that slaves and people on death row wear around their ankles. I thought of my mother's ankles, which I'd had to massage and which had forced her to give up classical dance. All the failure and misery of her life were contained in those ankles, and the pain must have ended up spreading through her whole body. Now I understood her better. He held out the cup to me again.

'Jasmine tea. I hope you like it.'

I must have looked pretty dreadful for him to be speaking so gently, almost in a whisper. I nearly asked him if I looked sick, but I couldn't bring myself to. I preferred not knowing.

'I get the impression that you're preoccupied by your childhood memories,' he said.

It all started with the woman wearing the yellow coat in the metro. Before that, I scarcely gave them a thought.

I swallowed a mouthful of tea. It was less bitter than the whisky.

He had got out his writing pad.

'You can trust me. I'm used to making sense of everything, even foreign languages, and yours is not that foreign to me.'

He seemed moved to have made this declaration. And I was moved, too.

'From what I can gather, you never found out who rented the huge apartment to your mother…'

I remember there was a cupboard in the living-room wall, at the spot where the steps covered in white plush formed a sort of dais. My mother would open the built-in cupboard and get out a wad of banknotes. I had also seen her give a wad to Jean Borand, one Thursday when he came to collect me. Apparently, there was enough in the treasure trove to last until the end, until the day she drove me to the Gare d'Austerlitz. Even that day, before I got on the train, she slipped an envelope into my suitcase; it contained several of those wads of notes. 'Give them to Frédérique, so that she looks after you.'

I wondered later where she had got hold of all that money. From the same man who had provided her with the apartment? The one whose name no one ever knew? Or what he looked like? Try as I might to dredge up a memory of him, I was sure I had never known any man who came as a regular visitor to the apartment. And it couldn't have been Jean Borand, since she was giving him money. Perhaps that fellow was my father, after all. But he didn't want to be seen;

he wanted to remain an unknown father. He must have come very late at night, around three in the morning, while I was asleep. I often woke in the middle of the night and, every time, I was sure I heard loud voices. My bedroom was quite close to my mother's. Twelve years later, I would have been curious to know how she felt, that first evening, when she arrived in the apartment, after leaving her hotel room in Rue d'Armaillé. Would she have felt that she was turning the tables on life? She had not been able to become a prima ballerina, and now, under a new identity, she wanted to have a role in a film by dragging me along with her, like a performing dog. And, from what I had gleaned at Frossombronne, listening to the conversations, it was the man whose name no one knew who had financed the film for her.

'Do you mind?'

He stood up and leaned over the radio. He turned a knob and the green light came on.

'I have to listen to a program tonight...For my work... But I've lost track of what time it starts.'

He turned the dial slowly, as if he was looking for a station that was difficult to tune into. Someone was speaking in a guttural language, and there was a long silence between each sentence.

'There—that's it.'

As the sentences followed, one after the other, he took notes on his pad.

'He's announcing the evening's programs...The broadcast I'm interested in is on later.'

I was pleased to see the green light. I don't know why, but I found it comforting, like those lights left on in the hall outside children's bedrooms. If they wake at night, they'll see light through the half-open door.

'Does it annoy you if I leave the radio on? I'm doing it just in case, to make sure I don't miss the program.'

Then I heard music, similar to the music I'd heard the other night when I was in the bedroom at Rue Coustou with the pharmacist. A pure, clear sound, conjuring the image of a girl sleepwalking across a deserted square at night, or the wind blowing down an esplanade in November.

'Is the background music annoying?'

'No.'

If I had been listening to it by myself, I would have found it depressing, but with him it didn't bother me at all. On the contrary, I found the music soothing.

'And do you still remember the address of the huge apartment?'

On the cover of my mother's diary, after the instruction: 'If lost, return this diary to…', I recognised her large handwriting: 'Comtesse Sonia O'Dauyé, PASSY 15 28.'

'I even remember the telephone number,' I told him.

I had dialled it so often from the booth in the café. One of the customers had commented that I was 'the little girl from 129'. It was late afternoon when I got home from Saint-André and no one came to answer the door. Neither my mother, nor the Chinese cook, nor his wife. The Chinese cook would get back around seven o'clock, but Comtesse Sonia O'Dauyé might not get back until the next day. Every time, I consoled myself that she hadn't heard the doorbell. She would definitely hear the phone ringing. PASSY 15 28.

'We could always try calling the number,' Moreau-Badmaev said, smiling.

In twelve years, the idea had never occurred to me. One day at Fossombronne, when I heard Frédérique say she'd gone once to Avenue Malakoff to collect some of my mother's belongings, I wondered what belongings she meant. The portrait by Tola Soungouroff? But she said she wasn't able to enter the apartment: there were red wax seals fastened onto the door. That night I dreamed that my mother had a burn mark on her shoulder, branded with a hot iron.

'PASSY 15 28, you said?'

He picked up the phone from the floor next to the bedside table and placed it on the bed. He held the receiver out to me and dialled the number. Back when I was living in the apartment, I had difficulty reading the letters and numbers on the dial in the phone booth at the café.

The ringing went on for a long time. It had an odd, muffled, reedy sound. Who might be living in the apartment now? The real owners, probably. The real children—the ones referred to on the board in the kitchen—had reclaimed the bedroom that I had no right to occupy for two years. And the real parents must be in the bedroom where my mother used to sleep.

'Seems like no one's answering,' Moreau-Badmaev said.

I held the receiver up to my ear. In the end, someone picked up, but no one answered. Men's voices, women's voices, voices from close by, voices from far away. They were trying to call each other and find a way to begin to answer each other. Every now and then, I distinctly heard two people talking to each other and their voices drowned out the others.

'The number is no longer in use. So people are using it to make contact and arrange to meet. It's called the Network.'

Perhaps all those unknown voices were individuals from my mother's diary whose telephone numbers didn't answer any longer. I could also hear a sort of rustling, the wind in the leaves, in summer, on Avenue Malakoff. I concluded that, since we had left, no one had lived in the apartment, except ghosts and these voices. The wax seals were still on the apartment door. The windows had been left wide open: that was why you could hear the wind. The electricity was off, like on the night of the air raid when I was so terrified that I ran to find my mother in the living room. She lit candles.

She didn't have many visitors. Two women often came: fat Madeleine-Louis and Simone Bouquereau. Later on, I saw them again in Frédérique's house in Frossombronne, but they avoided me and definitely didn't want to talk about my mother. Perhaps they were ashamed of something.

Simone Bouquereau had a head like a little blonde mummy, and I was shocked by how thin she was. The brunette said that Simone had 'been in rehab'. One evening, after dinner, she thought I had gone up to bed and she was talking about the past with Frédérique. 'Simone was the one who kept up poor Sonia's supplies,' she said. I wrote the words down on a scrap of paper. There were so many of their conversations I eavesdropped on, from the age of fourteen, in an attempt to understand. I asked Frédérique what it meant. 'Every now and again, ever since her accident, your mother took morphine.' I had no idea what accident she was referring to. Her ankles? Apparently morphine is a good cure for pain.

I still had the receiver up to my ear. The voices were drowned out by the rustling of the wind in the leaves. I pictured the wind slamming the doors and windows, blowing flurries of dead leaves onto the parquet floor and onto the steps covered in white plush in the living room; I imagined, too, the plush decayed and turned into moss, the glass in the windows broken; hundreds of cats overrunning the apartment, as well as black dogs, like the one she had lost in the Bois de Boulogne.

'Do you recognise someone's voice?' Moreau-Badmaev asked. He put the handset on the bed and smiled at me.

'No.' I hung up and put the telephone back on the floor. 'I'm frightened of going home by myself,' I said.

'But you can stay here.' He shook his head as if it was

obvious. 'I have to work now. I hope the noise of the radio doesn't disturb you.'

He left the bedroom, then came back with an old lampshade that he somehow attached to the tripod. The light from the globe became even more hazy. Then he sat on the edge of the bed, next to the radio, and placed the writing pad on his knees.

'The light isn't too strong for you?'

I replied that it was just right as it was.

I was lying on the other side of the bed, the side in shadow. On the radio, I heard the voice from earlier, just as guttural. Again, the silences between sentences. At intervals, he wrote words on his pad. I could no longer take my eyes off the green light and I drifted off to sleep.

ON WEDNESDAY, THE pharmacist was back from Bar-sur-Aube. I called her and she said we could get together in the evening. She suggested I meet her in her neighbourhood, but once again I was frightened of taking the metro and travelling across Paris by myself. So I invited her to have dinner in the café on Place Blanche.

I wondered what I could possibly do until evening. I didn't feel up to going back to Neuilly and looking after the little girl. What I most dreaded was walking along by the Bois de Boulogne, near the Jardin d'Acclimatation, around where the dog had gone missing. Almost every day, I used to go walking with the dog in the vicinity of the Porte Maillot. Luna Park was still there then. One afternoon, my mother asked me if I'd like to go to Luna Park. I thought she was going to take me. But no. When I think about it now, I imagine she just wanted me to leave her alone that afternoon. Perhaps she had a rendezvous with the man whose name no one ever knew and thanks to whom we were living in that apartment. She opened the built-in cupboard in the living-room wall, held out a big banknote. 'Go off and have fun at Luna Park,' she said. I had no idea why she was giving me so much money. She seemed so distracted that I didn't want to upset her. Outside, I considered not going to Luna Park. But when I got back she would probably ask me questions, demand that I show her the entry ticket or tickets for the rides. She often fixated on certain things and it was not worth trying to lie to her. And, anyway, at that time I didn't know how to lie.

When I bought my ticket at the entrance, the man seemed surprised that I was paying with such a large note. He gave me the change and let me through. It was a winter's day. So dark, it could have been night. In the middle of this funfair, I felt like I was in a bad dream. What struck me, above all, was the silence. Most of the stalls were shut. In the silence, the merry-go-rounds were working, but there was no one on the wooden horses. And no one walking around. I arrived at the base of the roller-coaster. The carriages were whizzing up and down the slopes at full speed, but they were empty. At the entrance to the roller-coaster, I saw three boys, older than me. They were wearing scruffy shoes that didn't match, with holes in them, and grey, torn overalls that were too short. They must have sneaked into Luna Park, because they were looking left and right, as if they were being followed. They seemed keen to get on the roller-coaster. I walked over to them and gave the biggest boy all the money I had left. And I ran away, hoping I'd be allowed to leave.

No, I wouldn't go to the Valadiers today, but I had to let them know. I left my room and walked to the post office on Place des Abbesses, after buying some paper and an envelope at Des Moulins *café-tabac*. I stood at one of the counters at the post office and wrote:

> *Dear Véra Valadier, I will not be able to come today to look after your daughter because I am ill. I would rather take it easy until Saturday when I will be at your place as usual at 4 in the afternoon. I apologise. Best wishes to Monsieur Valadier.*
>
> THÉRÈSE

I sent the letter by pneumatic post so that it would reach her in time. Then I went for a walk in the neighbourhood. The sun was shining and, as I walked along, I felt better. My breath came easily. I arrived at the edge of the Sacré-Coeur gardens, and I couldn't take my eyes off the cable car shuttling to and fro. I went back to my room in Rue Coustou. I lay on the bed and attempted, not for the first time, to read the book that Moreau-Badmaev had lent me. I began but, try as I might to battle my wandering mind, I kept returning to the first sentence, as if it were some sort of springboard from which I had to take the plunge. That first line has stayed in my mind: 'In general, life in the suburbs does not offer its inhabitants the level of comfort to which inner-city residents of large metropolises are accustomed.'

*

I had arranged to meet her at eight in the evening at the café in Place Blanche, the one that looks like a little house. There's a room on the first floor, but I had told her that I would be at one of the tables on the ground floor.

I got there half an hour early and chose a table near the bay window that looks out on Place Blanche. The waiter asked if I wanted to order a drink and I was tempted to get a whisky. But that would have been stupid: I didn't need it. I wasn't feeling the familiar weight pressing down on my chest. I told him I was waiting for someone, and just saying those few words did me as much good as any alcohol would have.

She entered the café at exactly eight o'clock. She was wearing the same fur coat as last time, and flat shoes. She caught sight of me immediately. As she walked to the table, I noticed that she carried herself like a dancer, but I found it more reassuring that she was a pharmacist. She kissed me on the forehead and sat next to me on the banquette.

'Are you feeling better than the other evening?'

She was smiling. There was something protective about the way she was looking at me, about that smile. I hadn't noticed that her eyes were green. I was too disoriented that Sunday in the armchair at the chemist, and later in my room the light hadn't been as bright as now in the café.

'I brought you something to give you a boost.'

From one of the pockets of her coat, which she had draped over the banquette, she fished out two bottles of medicine.

'Here's some cough mixture...you have to take it four times a day. And these are tablets to help you sleep. You take one at night, and whenever you feel a bit strange.'

She placed the two bottles in front of me on the table.

'And I think we should give you some injections of vitamin B12.'

All I could say was thank you. I would have liked to elaborate, but I wasn't used to being looked after, not since the nuns had been kind enough to make me inhale a pad doused in ether, the day I was knocked down by the truck.

Neither of us said anything for a moment. Even though I sensed that she would command respect in people, I had the feeling that she was just as shy as I was.

'You weren't a dancer, were you?'

She seemed surprised by my question, and then burst out laughing. 'Why?'

'Just before, I thought you walked like a dancer.'

She told me that, like most girls, she had taken dance lessons until the age of twelve, but nothing after that. I recalled another photo at the bottom of the biscuit tin. Two twelve-year-old girls wearing ballet outfits. Written in purple ink on the back of the photo, in a childish hand, were the words: 'Josette Dagory and Suzanne'—my mother's real first name. Jean Borand had the same photo stuck on the wall of his office in the garage. Everything was fine at the time of that photo. So when did the ankle accident happen, or the accident, full stop? How old was she? Now it was too late to find out. There was no one left to tell me.

When the waiter came over to our table, the pharmacist was surprised that I didn't order anything.

'You're so pale, you should eat something to build up your strength.'

Moreau-Badmaev had said the same thing, but she had more authority than he did.

'I'm not very hungry.'

'Well, you can share with me.'

I didn't dare contradict her. She put half of her meal on a plate for me and I forced myself to eat, my eyes shut, and counted the mouthfuls.

'Do you come here often?'

I used to go mostly in the mornings, very early, when the café opened; it was the time of day when I felt best. What a relief to be done with broken sleep and bad dreams.

'I haven't been back to this neighbourhood for ages,' she said. She pointed, through the bay window, at the chemist on the other side of Place Blanche. 'I worked there when I first started as a pharmacist. It was busier than where I am now.'

She might have come across my mother, after her 'accident', when she had a job as a dancer in this area, and still lived in a hotel room. The years are blurring in my head.

'I think there were a lot of dancers around here at that time,' I said. 'Did you know any?'

She frowned. 'Oh, you know, there was a real mix of people in the neighbourhood.'

'Did you work at night?'

'Yes. Often.' She was still frowning. 'I don't like talking about the past very much. You're hardly eating a thing. Don't be silly.'

I forced myself to eat one last mouthful to please her.

'Do you intend to stay in this neighbourhood for much longer? Couldn't you find a room a bit closer to the School of Oriental Languages?'

Of course, I had told her the other night that I was enrolled in the School of Oriental Languages. I'd forgotten that, in her mind, I was a student.

'I do plan on moving as soon as I can…'

I wanted to let her in on my secret: that the banquette I was sitting on then, in Place Blanche, was probably the same one my mother had sat on twenty years ago. And that, at the time of my birth, she was living, just like I was, in a room at 11 Rue Coustou, perhaps in my room.

'It's quite convenient for getting to the school,' I told her. 'I take the metro at Place Blanche and it's direct to Sèvres-Babylone.'

She had that sceptical smile again, as if she wasn't taken in by my lie. I was just saying whatever came into my head. I didn't even know where the School of Oriental Languages was.

'You look so anxious,' she said. 'I'd like to know what's worrying you.'

She brought her face up close to mine, those green eyes fixed on me the whole time. She wanted to read my mind; I would slip into a sweet drowsiness, talk without stopping, and come clean about everything. And she wouldn't need to take notes like Moreau-Badmaev.

'I'm going to stay for a bit longer in the neighbourhood, and then that will be the end of it.'

The more she fixed me with her green eyes, the more clearly I could see myself, as if I were a separate person from myself. It was quite simple: that evening, there is a girl with brown hair, scarcely nineteen, sitting on the banquette of a café in Place Blanche. You are five foot three inches tall, and you are wearing an off-white woollen cable-knit jumper. You're going to stay there a bit longer, and then that will be the end of it. You are there because you wanted to go back to the past one last time to try to understand. Right there, under the electric light, in Place Blanche, is where everything began. For one last time, you went back to your home country, to the beginning, to find out if there was a different path to take and if things could have turned out differently.

'What will it be the end of?' she asked me.

I made myself eat another mouthful to please her.

'You should have dessert.'

'No, thank you. But perhaps we could have a drink.'

'I don't think alcohol would be advisable in your case.'

I liked her sceptical smile and precise way of speaking.

'When was the last time you got out of Paris?'

I told her that I hadn't left Paris since I was sixteen, except for the two or three times when that fellow I'd known, Wurlitzer, took me to the beach on the North Sea.

'You should get some fresh air from time to time. Would you like to come with me on Saturday? I have to go to Bar-sur-Aube again for three days. It would do you good. I have a house just outside the town.'

Bar-sur-Aube. I pictured the first glimmer of sunlight, the dew on the grass, a walk along the river…Names alone set me dreaming.

She asked me again if I wanted to go with her on Saturday to Bar-sur-Aube.

'Unfortunately, I have to work in the afternoon,' I said. 'But I'm leaving around six in the evening.'

'Well, it might be possible. That's really very kind of you.'

I would ask Véra Valadier if I could leave earlier than usual. And what about the little girl? They probably wouldn't mind if I took her off for a few days to Bar-sur-Aube.

*

We walked along the median strip of the boulevard. I didn't dare ask her to stay with me again that night. I could still call Moreau-Badmaev. But what if, by chance, he wasn't at home and was busy somewhere else until tomorrow?

She must have sensed my anxiety. She took my arm. 'I can take you back to your place, if you'd like.'

We turned into Rue Coustou. And there, on the right, as we passed in front of the dark wooden façade of Zone Out, I saw a sign in the entrance: CINQ-VERNE, THE GIRLS AND

THE GHOST TRAIN. I remembered what Frédérique had said when she told me about my mother and the accident that forced her to give up ballet and work in places like this: 'A wounded racehorse on the way to the abattoir.'

'Are you sure you don't want to have a go on the ghost train?' the pharmacist asked. Her smile was comforting. In my room, she took the bottles of medicine out of one of the pockets of her coat and placed them on the bedside table.

'You won't forget? I've written the instructions on the bottles.' She leaned towards me. 'You're very pale…I think it would do you a lot of good to spend a few days outside Paris. There's a forest near the house where we can go for some lovely walks.'

She put her hand on my forehead.

'Lie down.'

I lay down and she told me to take off my coat.

'I have a feeling that right now I need to keep a close eye on you.'

She took off her fur coat, and laid it over me.

'You still don't have any heating. You'll have to come and spend winter in my apartment.'

She stayed sitting on the edge of the bed and again fixed me with her green eyes.

I GOT OFF the metro at Porte Maillot and followed the path that runs along the Jardin d'Acclimatation. It was cold but the sun was shining, and the sky was cloudless and blue, as it is perhaps in Morocco. All the shutters on the windows in the Valadier house were closed. Just as I was about to ring the doorbell, I noticed a letter stuck under the door. I picked it up. It was the letter I had sent on Wednesday, from the post office on Place des Abbesses. I rang the bell. No one answered.

I waited a while, sitting on the doorstep. The sun was blinding. I stood up and rang again. Then I told myself that it wasn't worth waiting any longer. They had left. The wax seals had probably been fastened to the doors. When I was there last, I had a hunch that would happen.

I held the letter in my hand. And I felt the vertigo coming back. It had been with me since I was young, since Fossombronne, when I used to try to cross the bridge. The first time, I ran; the second time, I walked fast; the third time, I made myself walk as slowly as possible to the middle. And now, once again, I had to try to walk slowly, away from the edge, saying comforting words to myself, over and over. Bar-sur-Aube. The pharmacist. *There's a forest near the house where we can go for some lovely walks*. I was walking down the path that runs along the Jardin d'Acclimatation; I was heading away from the house with the closed shutters. The feeling of vertigo was getting stronger and stronger. It was all because of the letter that had been stuck under the door for nothing and that no one would ever open. And yet I had sent it from the post office on Place des Abbesses, a post office like any other, in Paris, in France. The letters sent to me from Morocco must have stayed unopened like this one. A wrong address on the envelope, or a small spelling mistake, that's all it would have taken for them to go astray, one after the other, and end up in some unknown post office. Unless they'd been sent back to Morocco, but even then there was already no one there anymore. They'd gone missing, like the dog.

*

When I got out of the metro, the sun was still shining, the blue Moroccan sky. I went to the Monoprix in Rue Fontaine and bought a bottle of mineral water and a block of hazelnut milk chocolate. I crossed Place Blanche and took the short-cut down Rue Puget.

Back in my room, I sat on the edge of the bed, facing the window. I put the bottle of mineral water on the ground and the block of chocolate on the bed. I opened one of the bottles the pharmacist had given me and poured some of the pills into the palm of my hand. Little white pills. I put them in my mouth and swallowed them, along with a mouthful straight out of the bottle. Then I munched on a piece of chocolate. And repeated the procedure a few times. They went down better with the chocolate.

*

At first, I had no idea where I was. White walls and an electric light. I was lying on a bed that was not my bed from Rue Coustou. There was no pillow. My head was flat on the sheet. A nurse, a brunette, brought me some yoghurt.

She placed it a little way back, behind my head, on the sheet. She stood there, watching me. I said to her, 'I can't reach it.' She said, 'Give it a go. You need to make an effort.' She left. I burst into tears.

I was in a big glass cage. I looked around. There were aquariums in other glass cages. The pharmacist must have brought me here. We had arranged to meet at six o'clock in the evening to leave for Bar-sur-Aube. Inside the aquariums, I thought I could see shadows moving: fish, perhaps. I heard the noise of waterfalls, getting louder and louder. I had been trapped in icefields a long time ago, and now there was the gushing sound of them melting. I wondered what the shadows in the aquariums could possibly be. They told me later that there had been no more room, so they put me in the ward for premature babies. For a long time to come, I heard the noise of waterfalls, a sign that for me, too, from that day on, life was beginning.

PATRICK MODIANO, winner of the 2014 Nobel Prize in Literature, was born in Boulogne-Billancourt, France, in 1945, and was educated in Annecy and Paris. He published his first novel, *La Place de l'Etoile*, in 1968. In 1978, he was awarded the Prix Goncourt for *Rue des Boutiques Obscures* (published in English as *Missing Person*), and in 1996 he received the Grand Prix National des Lettres for his body of work. Mr. Modiano's other writings include a book-length interview with the writer Emmanuel Berl and, with Louis Malle, the screenplay for *Lacombe Lucien*.

PENNY HUESTON is an editor and translator.